Furthermore

Furthermore

SUSIE MAGUIRE

First published in Great Britain in 2005 by Polygon,
an imprint of Birlinn Ltd

West Newington House
10 Newington Road
Edinburgh
EH9 1QS

www.birlinn.co.uk

ISBN 10: 1 90459834 X
ISBN 13: 9 781904 598343

The publishers gratefully acknowledge subsidy from

Scottish
Arts Council

towards the publication of this volume

British Library Cataloguing-in-Publication Data
A catalogue record for this book is available on
request from the British Library

Design by James Hutcheson

Typeset by Palimpsest Book Production Limited,
Polmont, Stirlingshire
Printed and bound by Thomson
East Kilbride, Scotland

for my sister

Contents

Mae West Optional

A gull's feather falls out of the sky towards them like a toy propeller, black and grey and white, impossibly slowly. She scoops it out of the air as she offers the admission. He stops walking.

'You were scared of me? Why?'

'Because you're clever.'

'We're all clever in our own way. Clever isn't anything special.'

'No, you say that because you are. Intimidating. Huge intellect. Major reputation. Older man, all that. Made me feel like I was about fifteen.'

He snorts, shakes his head. He is intrigued by her wry tone, uncertain of her sincerity, their funny bones still not comfortably connected.

'Interesting to hear all this . . . my terrifying public persona.'

'Come on, you didn't know?'

'Well . . .'

'You don't notice people looking reverent? Quaking?'

'Sometimes. You seemed very confident. Quite cool.'

'Cool? Heavens.'

They walk along an empty beach, feet sinking in the wet sand right up at the edge of the sea. When water floods in fast she tugs him out of its path and looks back to see the tide wipe their tracks.

'Cool?' she says again. 'No. Magnetised, maybe. And you a master of observation.'

'I suppose I was too busy wondering if I was going insane.'

Now she laughs, a descending half-octave.

'From what?'

'Hmm.'

'Tell me.'

'Oh . . . From looking at you. Listening to you. Liking you.'

'Ah, the 'l' words. Good.'

They hold hands but let go again, in-touch and apart, conscious of the impermanence. Intimate strangers still assimilating the novelty of unexpected passion. Walking on a beach, as lovers do in expensive commercials or big-budget films, but walking in a capricious Scottish wind, fuelled by a night in a Scottish hotel, fatigued by full Scottish breakfasts. Amongst the bladderwrack and broken razor shells and lumps of sea-coal, an Irn-Bru can rolling in the foam boasts her national identity.

'So. Tell me more about how scary I am?' he requests, unaccustomed to the lightness in his own voice, the game.

'Oooh, you're so-o-o scary. I had to do that thing where you try to stop yourself being awed, so I imagined you in your underpants. But then suddenly I imagined you without your underpants. What a difference.'

He snorts again, slides a hand down her arm and cups her elbow. She stops to look at him. His grey-blue eyes, normally so focused and impersonal behind rectangular academic spectacles, now appear open to her. White hair blows forward onto his temples, flutters like downy feathers over his ears. His chin is firm, mouth straight and serious, a hint of austerity balanced by humour in the corners.

She circles a fingertip in the hollow above his shirt collar, then turns to regard the sea, and he turns with her. The water is grey-green up to a milky horizon, the sky piled with long, shredded white and grey cloud, like a dirty duvet. Wind blows up from the South-east as if there's a storm behind it.

'You come from a far-off land . . .'

Her intonation implies an epic journey, probably by camel train.

'England's quite nice in parts, you know.'

'Is Cambridge near the sea?'

'Geography has never entered your life, has it?' he teases.

'No reason to know anything about Cambridge. I'm not entirely provincial, if that's what you mean.'

'That's not what I mean.'

He glances at her profile, sees the small flicker of childish defensiveness. Her face is perhaps twelve years younger than his, barely lined by comparison. A sudden smile can smooth it free of tension as easily as the tide can erase marks on sand. He can't see himself yet, in her face. He wonders if they will have marked each other in any permanent way.

'Look.'

She points to the left side of the bay, where a small sailing boat is tacking past the tumble of fallen cliff. A tiny figure in the bow is immobile, another in red with a bright yellow life jacket is hauling at sheets and the canvas pulls tight. She sighs, captivated by the image, two people at sea, bound for unknown shores, all the clichéd metaphors.

'Beautiful. Do you know how to sail?'

'Never been on a dinghy like that. My sons like boats, the eldest one rows . . .'

She turns her face to him for a look which expresses no more than a civil, guarded interest in his other life, and his whole body floods with regret and confusion at having spoken.

'I'm sorry.'

'Don't. You can't be sorry. Children are facts.'

She doesn't add, *and you have a wife whom you love despite this temporary folly*, trying to keep that part of it still inside the bubble.

'I am sorry. I said I didn't want to hurt you.'

No way to avoid that, she thinks. It would have hurt to walk away, too. It will hurt tomorrow when he leaves, it will go on hurting until it stops hurting. This kind of hurt and the joy are inseparable until we notice them, name them. But silence and touch are the only answers she can offer, and she leans in, her brow butting under his chin like a cat, nudging him from reflection to action. He holds her body almost politely at first, then returns her embrace, pulling her so close she can feel the air leaving his lungs, feel his shirt buttons as individual pressure points, little weapons against her skin. Sacred pain. The words come into her head and she says them quietly. He seeks her mouth for a kiss which goes from tender to hungry in sixty seconds.

He remembers their meeting in every detail. A reception room filled with people. The young women amidst the gathering caught his eye fleetingly, admiration for their physical grace, no more than habit, but his attention was suddenly snared by her laugh, and then the slow turn of her head as she surveyed the room. And the pause. The pause as she looked directly at him. Her lips still moving in conversation with the friend but her face still, for a few long seconds more, then a smile, the eyelids came down and she looked away. With her back to him he couldn't remember any features except the eyes slowly seeing him, gripping him.

He asked to be introduced, casually. Close up, her face was not particularly beautiful, but humorous, animated by a curious, intelligent perception. Her chin came up as she shook his hand, fine dark hair fell across her eyes and she pushed it back, and she spoke very quickly in the noisy room so that he found himself stooping a bit to catch every word, straightening when he replied, a repeated action like the courtship dance of some exotic bird of paradise.

He can rationalise, now, having spent more time in her gaze, that the shock of that first visual experience was in part his own projection, some acute flutter of loneliness and middle-aged susceptibility, and in part the purely physical components of her face, the way the large eyes sit under her brows, the way they react to light, the dark rings around the very blue irises. He knows that reading a face is subjective, though after fifteen hours in her company he also believes that her particular face reflects character supremely. Now, he looks into it again to seek the compelling interest he had felt radiate across the room. Her struggle to smile makes him falter.

'I like your face,' he said. 'Why did you like mine?'

'I've always liked yours. In photos, on book jackets and so on, though they always look too stern, I think. It's different now, though.'

She was interested before she saw him, admired his work, was aware of his professional reputation, and connecting that with his physical presence pushed her curiosity into the red zone. In childhood, her mastery of the upturned glass and the lexicon of letters in playful family séances led to accusations of cheating, ferociously denied. Later she preferred to see it as her first experiment in mind over matter, a parlour trick in which she had asserted a dominance that never materialised on the sports field or in the classroom.

Spotting his celebrated features at the reception and looking boldly at him, every particle of her energy focused, was something like the same trick, and she felt briefly ashamed of her blatancy until she detected a matching intensity, veiled by caution but undeniable. Conversation, then a drink, dinner. A friend's voice in her head: *if you have to look at the price tag, you probably can't afford it.* She is as honest with herself as she knows how to be, so when the possibilities lit up in a dazzling sequence she wanted them all, everything, greed overruling reason, and didn't hide it.

'Different . . . because you've inspected me pore by pore?'

'Yes. You don't scare me any more. At a molecular level you're only human.'

Again that deliberate, ironic twist.

'You scare me.'

'Ha!'

She seizes his hand and hauls him into motion. Within a few steps she detaches, bends to pick up a stone, oval and pink with veins of white, hands it to him. Another one, grey with yellow splotches, oxidised iron. She gives him that one, too. A third, not stone but glass, smooth and blue, no bigger than a fingernail. She folds his fingers over them deliberately, one by one, wraps her hands around his fist, keeping her eyes on the knot of fingers.

'Take these for your cabinet of curiosities.'

'I'll make a space for them.'

'Good.'

She walks on, finding more stones for herself, skimming the flat ones, and he follows, wondering if she really thinks he would forget her without these innocent keepsakes. He has already burned the images of their time together onto his memory where they are noisily clashing with conscience. He will relive them privately, at home. The familiarity of Cambridge, his study, the hand-carved shelf above the computer. These new tokens arranged not too close to the photo of his wife and sons, taken on last summer's holiday in Maine. Mark and Alun and Oona on a bench under a tree, faces brown and animated, six long, tanned legs stretched out together as they leant back in laughter, chorusing 'Monterey Jack' for the camera. He drops the three gifts into his pocket. The clunk clink clack as they touch his dormant mobile phone reminds him to look at his watch. His plane leaves in two hours.

She is thinking about the end now. All the covenants one person might make to another are not to be voiced, not by her. She wants to think ahead to when she will remember, without embarrassment or self-loathing, that she didn't ask for anything other than to be present until he would be absent. She paces ahead of him, hands in pockets, towards the path to the parking area, where the roof of her car gleams silver through the dunes. She will drive him back to the hotel, where the concierge will book him a taxi to the airport. His wife will expect to see a receipt for that when she reminds him to submit his expenses.

He registers the first tug of loss as she strides on, hair flapping raggedly behind her over the collar of her blue jacket. Better loss than regret, perhaps. His gaze returns to the sea. The sky is closing in, darker clouds sweeping in almost as fast as the tide has turned. Water rushes up the sand, sucking and hissing until all their footprints are gone. Standing a moment longer on the shore he watches the dinghy, until it tacks out of sight on the far side of the broad bay, heading for harbour.

Nice Puppies

'What kind of dog are you looking for?'

'Don't know. A bitch, definitely. Maybe a setter.'

'Naw. Setters, spaniels and that, they just walk out of here the minute they arrive. Some other lonely wee face'll leap out at you. You're passed on the paperwork, yeah?'

'I've been vetted.'

The volunteer's white wellies had the name *Ewan* written down the back in smudged red marker. Carla followed them along a wet concrete pathway towards the canine prison camp, which was broadcasting a frenzied symphony of barks, yelps and whimpers. Ewan ushered her into the enclosure and left her to browse. The abandoned dogs were so eager to love someone that she had to spend ages wandering from kennel to kennel, gradually hardening her heart against fluffy mongrels and grey muzzles. Then she found a smooth-haired black and tan dachshund bitch not long out of puppyhood, a recent arrival. At the sight of its ginger eyebrows circumflexed above the pointed black face, Carla was won over.

'Hope you and Sindy are gonnae be happy together,' Ewan chirped as he handed Carla the dog's leash, and held open the door from the office to the car park.

'She's going to be called Eva now,' said Carla. 'You know, like Eva Braun?'

'Oh aye? Very nice,' said Ewan.

Carla positioned the dog's bed under her drawing desk so that Eva could be close while she worked on her illustration commissions, took Eva to the local park twice a day, bought her biscuit treats and squeaky toys for training, and cuddled her while they watched TV. As Carla wept at Carrie Bradshaw's disappointments in love, Eva laid a consoling paw on her chest and licked her chin.

When the mercurial spring weather made her restless in the city, Carla took Eva to a favourite beach. The sky was grey, and wind whipped the sea into dirty froth like weak cappuccino. Carla huddled in a pea-green coat on a driftwood log and watched Eva snuffling and scraping in the wet sand, the dog's tiny pawprints not much bigger than seagull tracks. Her gaze on Fife's distant refineries, Carla didn't notice the approaching runners until they were very close, and screamed involuntarily as a boxer dog pounded towards Eva with loud huffing noises. Eva wagged her tail frantically as the big dog loomed over her.

'Eva, come here! Come, Eva!'

'Benny, sit!'

The boxer's owner slowed to a walk, cast a glance in Carla's direction, then went to his dog which was keenly sniffing Eva's hindquarters.

'Benny!'

The boxer squatted slowly, its bottom still technically clear of the sand, and turned its squashy face apologetically towards the man, who grabbed it by the collar. Belatedly, Eva started to bark and prance, ears flapping. Carla picked her up and shooshed her. The boxer's owner fondled its bony head.

'Sorry if we gave you a fright. He wouldn't have hurt her.'

'Well, you never know.'

'No, he's really a softie, aren't you pal? Eh? A big softie . . .'

His hands smoothed Benny's coat, but his eyes were on her face. Their talk was outwardly casual but it took him only twelve minutes to reveal that his name was Matt, that he was an insurance executive, that his dog was named after the famous Scottish boxer Benny Lynch, and to suggest they meet for a drink some night. Flattered by his confidence, Carla agreed to a midweek lunch instead, and watched Matt jog away, Benny loping beside him, their rears uniformly pert. Carla had never believed in that thing about owners resembling their dogs, and had never cared for boxers, hound or human, but she noticed parallels between the dog's butch stance and the man's, and found it perversely attractive.

The first night Matt slept with her, Carla shut her bedroom door despite Eva Braun's pitiful protest. The whimpering quickly became intrusive, and Carla got up to quiet the dog. When she came back to Matt, sprawled across the bed, he asked,

'How d'you get her to stop?'

'I gave her a rubber bone she likes.'

'Really. Let me offer you something similar, young lady . . .'

Though she winced at his banter, she didn't refuse. His body was muscular, tasted salty and smelled good, and when she bit his shoulder he growled comically, so she did it again. He paid a lot of attention to her breasts and later, as they lay curled together, he continued to touch them.

'You're a chest man, then?' she asked.

'Not particularly. Yours are nice, though.'

'Small,' she said, 'not that I'm apologising.'

'Nothing wrong with wee dugs,' said Matt, rolling them under his palms.

When Matt left in the morning, Carla stripped the bed, filled the espresso machine, and did her face; moisturiser, concealer, mascara, lipstick. She combed her hair sleek into its Dorothy Parker bob, taking a moment to snip at the coppery fringe where it threatened her eyebrows. Then she called her sister.

'A rubber bone? For God's sake, Carla!'

'Not the worst description I've heard.'

'Spare me the others, then. So, how was it?'

'Good. Pretty good. Further research needed.'

'Uh-huh . . . is he a nice guy, though?'

'Yeah. A bit literal. A bit coarse. Funny, though, he's quite like his dog, all testosterone and attitude on the outside . . .'

'Oh? Did he howl?'

'Fiona, shut your face. I might really like him.'

'Well, good. Hurry up and marry him and live happily ever after.'

'I don't want to get married and I have got a life . . .'

'You've got a sausage dog and a mortgage, I wouldn't call that a life.'

During the months that followed, Carla saw Matt often. They met in the early evening to exercise their dogs in the park, spent long weekends together walking at the beach or cooking at home, bought each other presents, learned each other's habits. The dogs grew friendly and playful, nipping and chasing in long, tongue-lolling romps which usually ended with Eva on her back in submission and

Benny, over-excited, pinning her to the ground with his floppy wet muzzle. Of the four, the humans were the prettier couple, the dogs the least concerned with relationship etiquette. Discussion on families, religion, politics, children and, of course, contraception had been conducted between Carla and Matt on a pretty informal basis, neither willing to talk commitment first, but Matt betrayed a huge romantic streak which made Carla glow.

They planned to celebrate their three-month anniversary, the midsummer weekend, at Matt's place, the ground floor of an old Georgian house with a kitchen-cum-conservatory opening onto a mature private garden. On Friday night they cooked dinner together, drank champagne and made love tenderly. Carla heard Matt offer the words 'love you' in a furtive groan, and she whispered it back with a rush of gratitude. Matt fell asleep quickly. Carla lay awake thinking about the future. She pictured herself in various scenarios, announcing their engagement to her sister, her parents. She considered honeymoon possibilities. It all seemed feasible.

Restless from her forward planning, she got up to go to the bathroom. Matt's pale green bath-towels had fallen to the floor, and one sported a boxer-sized pawprint, so she tipped open the laundry hamper. The edges of a magazine emerged from under the small bundle of shirts and she pulled it out. The cover featured a young blonde woman with heavy breast implants, under the bold, red title XL. Inside, more of the same, and worse. Straps, buckles, implements. Carla pushed the magazine back under the soiled clothes, sat on the edge of the bath. She listened to her brain debate feminist principles, attraction and revulsion, insecurities about her own body. She cried a little, looked at her breasts in the mirror, judging them. She wrapped herself in a clean t-shirt from the airing cupboard and crept back to Matt's bed, where sleep came slowly.

Saturday afternoon started as Matt had planned it. He set out deck chairs in the sun, and was deep into the latest Brookmyre novel, turning the pages with an impatient flick. Carla lay with her eyes closed, feigning sleep. She was exhausted and intensely irritable. Eva lay panting in the shadows under the rhododendrons. Benny was shut in the house, in disgrace for having coupled with Eva who had, quite unexpectedly, come into season overnight, and whose loud yelps had woken Carla at 7 a.m. and had her running into the kitchen in panic.

The mating was grotesque. Eva's small body rested on her front paws, her hips elevated by Benny's thrusts, their toenails clicking against the tiles as they danced an intimate tango. Carla had scolded them, drenched them in cold water, smacked Benny's rump, but the dogs were firmly bonded. Matt had staggered through from the bedroom naked, his own erection bobbing like a dowsing rod. When he laughed Carla wanted to hit him.

'It's not funny, he's hurting her!'

'She'll be all right! Carla, calm down.'

'She won't be all right, look at the size of her, think about it!'

'Nature has its way, you know? I mean . . . you know?'

'I'm calling the vet, we've got to get them apart . . .'

'You'd be better coming back to bed and leaving them to it.'

He nuzzled her neck, put his hands under her t-shirt and pressed her nipples. She moved away from him to the phone, punched in 192 and got the number of the dog pound. When she got through to the vet on call he suggested she separate the dogs – as soon as feasible – and bring Eva in on Monday to find out why she hadn't been routinely spayed.

The rest of the morning had been awkward. Carla knew it had as much to do with the magazine she'd found as with what she perceived to be the violation of her dog. Benny was shut in the spare bedroom, the garden was humming with bees and butterflies and rich with the smell of flowers, and Eva looked perfectly relaxed, twisting her belly up to roll her back against the cool earth. Carla saw only beauty in Eva's abandonment, repulsion when she pictured herself, belly-up to Matt the night before. Anniversary paradise lost.

Matt flicked through another page and she felt her control snap.

'What is it with men and breasts, anyway?'

'Pardon?'

'You said you liked them. Liked mine. And I found your dirty magazine.'

Matt closed the book slowly and shifted to look at her, his expression blank.

'I do. They're nice, they're part of you. The photos are just photos, it doesn't mean anything, Carla. It's nothing to do with you . . .'

Carla's brain knotted. Unable to articulate her conflicting thoughts as emotion heaved in her throat, she got up and hauled Eva out from under the bush. The dog bumped against her hip as she stalked indoors, ignoring Matt, who was calling her name with increasing exasperation. She tugged her crepe dress over her bikini, picked up her bag and Eva, and drove home holding back tears. The first thing she did after slamming the door was unplug the phone.

On Monday morning, the middle-aged vet was more practical than sympathetic.

'What kind of dog was it?'

'A boxer. Do you think she's pregnant?'

He sucked air over his teeth.

'Better to be safe than sorry. They'd be big pups, and she's a very small bitch. Pity not to let her have a first litter, but it would be asking for trouble. They'd be ugly little mutts anyway.'

He offered an appointment to have Eva spayed, and Carla agreed before he'd finished his sentence.

Matt wrote to her, two pages of hand-scrawled apology mixed with indignation and affectionate reproach, slid through her letterbox on Sunday night. She read it and cried and read it again but didn't phone him. Another envelope arrived midweek containing the offending porn magazine, thoroughly machine-shredded. He sent red roses on Friday, and turned up at her flat on Saturday morning as she was coming back from shopping. As she put her key in the lock he called her name. She got the door open, turned and looked at him from behind her sunglasses. He walked towards her, his hands open and loose at his sides. He was wearing her favourite green shirt.

'Please let me talk to you, Carla, I need to know what's going on.'

'I don't want to talk.'

'That's pretty selfish, isn't it? I've apologised. You just walk out and I'm supposed to guess what's happening?'

She shrugged. He shook his head, put his hands on his hips.

'Don't do this. You know I love you, you know that.'

From the back seat of Matt's Saab, Benny stared up at

her, slobbering over the edge of the partially open window. Suddenly the man-and-his-dog picture gelled. She looked at Matt's muscular neck and arms, the way he stood, the strength in his hands, and she felt sick.

'I don't want to see you any more,' said Carla.

'Oh come on!'

'No. It's over.'

'No. I don't accept that. I don't accept that!'

Suddenly his face went from normal to red and angry. She stepped inside and slammed the door, bolted it, heart pounding as she heard him run up the steps, heard him shout in total disbelief and fury, 'You bitch! You arrogant fucking bitch!' She vomited before she could reach her bathroom.

Her young GP was more sympathetic than the vet had been.

'These early tests aren't always reliable, but we'll see. How far along do you think you might be?'

'I'm a week late. But I've also been pretty upset . . .'

'Emotional distress can sometimes cause disruptions to the menstrual cycle. Do you want to be pregnant?'

'No. No. God. I don't know.'

'How about your partner?'

The doctor's smile came with a little querying frown, her eyes flicking from Carla's face to the test kit to her sensible wristwatch and back.

'That's . . . irrelevant.'

'I see. Have you thought about termination? I can arrange that for you.'

Carla felt a giddiness flood her, a cold feeling like the aftermath of a hangover. She pressed a hand to the bridge of her nose and leaned back into the chair. Then the doctor was telling her to lean forward, put her head between her knees, the woman's hand firm and warm against her neck, and she stared at the woman's shoes, fawn suede sandals with blue-varnished toenails peeping through at the tips. Five little piggies go to market, she thought. Five ugly little mutts.

'Only another minute now,' said the doctor. 'Just relax.'

The Laws of Motion

The house was quiet at last. The floorboards had ceased to creak beneath the pounding of children's feet, the doors stood silently ajar, the television was mute. She could hear her own breathing. Beyond the window, rain dripped ceaselessly as it had since the previous night, a curtain across the real world, enclosing her behind misted glass. Head in hand at the kitchen table, she drew her finger through the breakfast crumbs, divided the milk puddles absentmindedly with the back of a knife.

When the letterbox flapped she got up and looked out of the kitchen to the front door. Brown envelopes and circulars spewed across the hall floor. She ignored them. In the bedroom, where the curtains now tinted the room a deep glowing red, she crawled back into bed, drew the quilt up to her ears, and shut her eyes.

She could still hear their voices in her head, clamouring for bus money, missing socks, a vital calculator. Turn them off. Beside the bed, her book lay open on the floor, spine cracked where she'd stepped on it, struggling with slippers in the dark a couple of hours ago. Its shiny cover promised romance and adventure, but it had failed to deliver. She was using it simply as a shield, the lines of letters slid beneath her eyes, shut out anxiety, soothed nerves, while whatever sense they were intended to convey evaporated. She might as well read the same book forever, start it afresh each time; she'd still be unable to focus on its plot or its characters. Her mind was briefly engaged by the author's detailed references to sex and food, appetites long forgotten pricked briefly into life, leaving her ashamed.

Sleep, then. Sometimes she slept all day, only waking when the children put their key in the lock at 4 p.m., to stagger from the bedroom confused, sweaty, head thick and aching. The children were aware of, but had ceased to remark upon, her condition. Perhaps they talked of it at school with friends: 'Hey, my Mum's a zombie.'

Her mind was divided, opposed, on the subject of motherhood, its challenges, its rewards, her inability to take satisfaction in either. In the mornings, the part of her that still functioned, that small voice, told her to get dressed, go out, swim, join a group, hold a coffee morning. Who would she ask? Those brightly dressed mothers who still met their kids after school, who gathered at the gates discussing Parents' Association business, Halloween parties, arrangements for weekend sleepovers? She had given up on that long ago. The lethargy overwhelmed her. What clothes ought she to wear? She might be eligible for free swimming, but it was miles to the pool and besides, she couldn't carry shopping home tired from a swim. Couldn't spend money on a swimsuit, couldn't bare her white skin. Often there was nothing in the house to eat. In the supermarket, she didn't seem to be able to choose, stomach protesting as she passed the deli counter, revolted by the sight of the sweaty yellow cheeses, the glistening pink coils of sausage.

A packet of tea, milk, some digestives. Supper for the kids out of cans which pulled at her shoulders during the long walk home. She should get a trolley, she should ask for a lift from a neighbour, she should do a lot of things. She felt incapable.

Her GP had been impersonally jovial, briskly interrogative, finally patriarchal. She'd pull out of it, medication could help the depression, perhaps if she had some practical help, family? She shook her head. 'The father is out of the picture, I take it? A friend, then?' She almost smiled at that. Another man, he meant. Who would want her, like this? Who did she ever meet, anyway? 'I'm not who you think I am!' she wanted to shout at him.'You have no idea how I live!'

Under the covers she dreamed. Her ex-husband walked into the room demanding to know what she had done with his time. Where had she put it? She ran barefoot through the rooms of their old house, looking in cupboards, under newspapers, in the fridge, calling to him not to worry, she would find it. Time became an animal, she felt its warm breath at her back, saw its tail whisk out of reach under the bedroom door. Her husband sat at the kitchen table, gravy dripping down his shirt and tie. She turned to fetch a wet cloth and found herself in a vast garden, raking autumn leaves, wearing a cardigan she knew she didn't possess, the colour of brambles and cream, with large glass buttons. Her husband was throwing her pyjamas onto the bonfire. She knew she was dreaming. Ghosts often came to torment her in these dreams, and she struggled to wake up, shouting 'No!', pushing them away, but they always came back.

She was woken by the phone, but didn't pick up, predicting it would cease the minute she put her hand on it. Soon, pressure on her bladder forced her out of bed. The dreary whirring of the bathroom extractor fan made her frown, the frown told her to take some painkillers, go out, breathe oxygenated air. She pulled on her warmest coat, and a baseball cap one of the kids had found in the park. Her stomach growled with hunger. In the streets, the drizzle continued, but she found it freshening, and turned her face into it. Perhaps she should close her eyes, feel her way just by the soft wetness on her cheeks, the taste of rain in her mouth and nose, like a hound on the scent. She imagined herself a mongrel, lean beneath a shaggy multi-coloured coat, collarless, passing the day padding from smell to smell.

When the rain stopped so did she, finding herself outside the museum. In the foyer there was a floor plan of exhibits, arrows pointing to a café. Threading her way through rooms full of armour, scenes from civil war history, she felt in her pockets for change, enough for a bowl of soup. The café was quiet, and she sat alone spooning salty pea and ham, her eyes roaming the walls between mouthfuls, returning to fix on the spray of pink carnations in front of her. The flowers were real, but they represented an illusion. Spring wasn't here, spring existed in a warm plastic-covered tunnel somewhere that forced these delicate blooms. Somewhere, child labourers went blind, became infertile, due to the chemicals sprayed onto plants to produce spring any time for hospital patients, presentation bouquets, cheap table arrangements.

She abandoned the soup, wandered through the galleries, passing beneath huge dusty oil paintings, and the gaze of long-dead women who regarded her with tolerance and amusement, patience and serenity. In the Roman section, a glint of copper caught her attention, jewellery from a burial mound. She halted in front of a skull, the bone brown with age, the teeth almost perfect. Her eyes refocused, catching her own face superimposed in the glass of the cabinet. She looked at herself and death for a long time. In the reflection, her pulled-back hair, dark, deep-set eyes, shadows in the hollows of her face, made the similarities apparent. She took off the cap, shook her hair free from its plait until it rippled over her shoulders. The length startled her, her hair a living healthy thing even when she ignored it.

'Molly?' A tentative question, then a hand on her arm. 'Molly, how've you been? How are the kids? I've tried to call you but you're never in, woman; get an answering machine, for heaven's sake!' Kath gave her a strong hug, a kiss on the cheek, and stood back, smiling.

Molly – when had she last heard anyone call her by her name? She smiled back, unable to formulate an answer. The warmth of Kath's greeting overwhelmed her, she almost flung herself back into the embrace, just to feel it again. Suddenly there was either so much to say – or nothing. She shook her head, laughed, a stopgap. *Kath, I spend my days in limbo, wishing to be somewhere else, someone else, help me, or walk away and leave me before I cry my heart out to you.* She couldn't find a way into natural conversation, her cheeks ached from smiling, an internal clock counted the seconds since the question, and she sought Kath's eyes again. Kath's expression was animated, open, happy. Molly indicated the skull, laughed nervously. 'I've been dead.' Kath pursed her lips. 'No, no, pale, but definitely still breathing.' They both laughed. Kath gripped Molly's hands.

'God, it's great to see you Moll. How long has it been? A year anyway, no, must be longer, look at the length of your hair. You used to have it shoulder-length, didn't you?'

'Yeah, well, saves money, growing it. How are you, how's . . .'

'Fine, everything's fine, Evan's got a new job, I'm still trying to change the world through community video, we bought a car, di-dah di-dah.' Kath gripped Molly's hands again. 'Listen, what are you doing right now? Because we've got to catch up, but I'm getting a haircut in about five minutes round the corner from here. Hey, d'you want to come with me? Look . . .' She dug into her jacket pocket and took out a printed card. *Hair cut or coloured for half normal price, or bring a friend for free.* It's a new place, they might not be busy, maybe we could get done together, eh? A wee bit of pampering. C'mon, let's do it.'

Something leapt inside her. Was it fear, was she scared to change her routine? Kath's energy was a beacon to which Molly felt inexorably drawn, the chance flash of a light-house on a dark night, reaching out to bring her comfort. And yet she had never thought to phone Kath, never counted her as a proper friend. Molly needed more of this. She felt herself suddenly addicted, afraid, poised on the brink of saying no and finally saying nothing, nodding, letting herself be steered out into the street.

The sky was clearing, grey sheets moving westward, fat white clouds coming in from the coast with a glint of sun. The wind tossed her loose hair, stroked her scalp, as she walked with Kath up the road and into the new salon. The place looked expensive, but not intimidating. Molly was shampooed by a junior who massaged her hair to the rhythm of Radio 1, asking, 'So, what are you getting done today?' Molly replied, 'I don't know. I haven't really looked at myself for about three years.'

The stylist, a woman of her own age, slim in cream linen

skirt and toffee-coloured silk shirt, asked her the same question, combing her hair this way and that. Molly glanced around at the salon walls, where black and white photographs promised immortal perfection, and then back at herself, dishevelled and shabby.

'I'd like it very short, not all over, but, well, just anything you want.'

The scissors rapidly took care of the bulk, gleaming snakes falling to the floor where they were swept aside by the junior. Her head tilted forward, sideways, her vision tantalisingly blocked by locks of damp, scented hair, Molly watched herself revealed. Across the room, in the mirror, she could see Kath's neat chestnut head shaping up under the hands of a tiny woman wearing platform clogs. Molly used the trick of unfocusing her gaze until the drying process started, her hair teased into curves and spikes. Holy cow, she looked like kd lang. With every lift of her hair, her eyes appeared to grow larger, her face more balanced. When it was done she regarded her image squarely, discovering a firm chin, strong, graceful neck, definite eyebrows and suddenly interesting cheekbones. She was forced to admit to herself that she might be beautiful. Why was that so hard, so embarrassing? It came to her that her beauty had never been for herself before, that she'd waited for approval from others and placed no value on her own opinion. This new Molly was her, was the old Molly given back to her, as she had been before divorce and exhaustion, or as she might have been had life been different. There was less similarity to the skull than she'd imagined.

Molly slipped on her coat and stuffed the cap into her pocket, while Kath paid the receptionist. The effect of the change in appearance, as she moved through the mirrored salon, made her heart thud with an excitement she didn't yet recognise as liberation; from the immediate past, from the constant dullness in her spirit. Outside the breeze picked up her hair and played with it, lifting Molly's mood still higher. A kind of giddiness overtook her, as it did sometimes in dreams, and as they walked up the street she flung her arm round Kath's shoulder and squeezed, and Kath turned and hugged her, rocked her, so that they stood there swaying, practically dancing together, as the traffic splashed past.

'I've got to get back to work now, Moll.'

'Oh, sorry, listen, thanks, really . . .'

'Ah, shut up, it was a pleasure – now promise me something.' Kath took her by the collar of her coat and gave her a mock ferocious look, 'Promise you'll call, any time, I want to hear from you. Bring the kids round, and we'll all go out for a day, or just you and me, okay?' Molly nodded.

Kath walked away through a crowd of office workers, turning once to wave quickly and to make a face about overheard comments from the men, a huddle of would-be executives, which made Molly laugh out loud and feel suddenly the centre of attention, standing still in the middle of the pavement as the blue-grey sea of 'suits' parted and passed her by with curious sidelong glances. She felt so different that even their gaze didn't raise her hackles as it might have, and she turned on her heel, walking back through them, pushing, 'Excuse me', and pacing out in front, tossing her head.

Her legs felt as light as her mood, so she ran across the road, ignoring cars, and went straight through the revolving door of a department store. She prowled the cosmetics counters, picked up a lipstick and applied it, a rich creamy terracotta. When the polyurethaned assistant hastened towards her, Molly skipped away, and began opening all the tubes and pots on the next display, squeezing colour lavishly onto her skin, smearing tribal stripes across the backs of her hands. Two atomisers, randomly chosen, created a perfumed mist for her to drift through. In an enlarging mirror she powdered her face ghostly white, drew black lines round her eyes, transforming her face into an oriental mask. When she turned to leave people were staring, mouths hanging open, whispering. A little girl holding her mother's hand pointed and laughed. She smiled back at them all, a model's smile become fierce, and danced towards the lift. It took her as far as the fourth floor; restaurant, carpets, bedding. Striding past the linens, she had the sensation that she was moving faster than anybody else, leaving people standing like passengers at a station when the express train hurtles through. Exhilarated, she wanted to go further, faster, higher. In the short corridor to the ladies', an open window let in the rain-scrubbed air, and she stuck her head through it to breathe deeply.

Immediately below and to the left, a slate roof rose towards the sky like a small-scale ski-slope, inviting exploration. She pushed up the window jamb, pulling herself up until she could swing one knee onto the lintel and crawl out onto the roof. She wanted a clear view of the sky. The light was changing, moving towards dusk, with most of the shop windows lit up like advent calendars. Stretching out her arms for balance she made her way slowly up to the crest of the roof, looking down at her feet, placing them carefully one in front of the other, as though measuring the journey. The wind tugged at her coat, tickled her nose, sang in her ears. She sang back to it, wordlessly. When she was within reach, she grasped a chimneystack and looked up; straight up above her, a huge metal globe hovered, a wind-vane of sorts, speared by a sturdy rod. She climbed higher until she could reach its base, could wrap her arms around the world, resting her chin on its coldest bronze continent. Below, the world was turning; up here it was still, it had stopped for her to make observations.

She took in a deep breath and expelled it in a shout, an exultant whoop which caused a flurry of beating wings, as the pigeons of the city rose into panicked flight, circling, soaring, wheeling around her like stars. Feet firmly planted, she shrugged out of the heavy layers of her clothing until she was bare to the waist, the chill air raising goose-bumps, and lifted her arms to the sky, taking handfuls of it, imprinting upon it her shape, her spirit, a living sculpture, a tiny netsuke. Far below, humans crawled along the street, oblivious to the displacement of air her movements made, the delicate alterations to the turning of the globe effected by her every gesture.

To Boldly Go

A MARINA McLOUGHLIN STORY

I have always really really really wanted to travel. To travel round the world, broadening my mind. I've always loved the idea of journeys, because of books where people do it so grandly. When Evelyn Waugh or Agatha Christie wrote about going somewhere exotic by ship of train or car, they never worried about their luggage, there was always a porter. As a tourist, in those days, you could just shove on a pith helmet, your stout walking shoes, waggle your forked stick and step off the steamer or the Orient Express or whatever, and expect to be followed by hordes of cheerful native bearers.

I'm not saying it was politically correct, but it stopped you getting sore arms. I hate luggage. I'd rather die than have to carry a suitcase any distance. Of course, in theory, travelling light is okay, with maybe only a change of clothes; it's fine, as a concept, but I just bet the one pair of jeans you'd packed would be too tight by the time you'd reached Mombasa or Alice Springs or wherever. And the other thing about actual travel, it's okay if you're immune to everything or you drink seven bottles of whisky a day, but if it was me, I'd get flu just when I set foot out the front door, or my hair would annoy me, or I'd get really homesick, all things which sort of ruin the experience of going abroad. In fact, I'd probably have a mental fit right there in the customs hall and be hospitalised for extreme exhaustion and total insanity. Best to have it in UK Customs. In foreign hospitals you probably wouldn't get jelly, like you do here, when you're feeling a bit ill.

Also, I can't stand mosquitoes and tsetse flies and big spiders and stuff, so that pretty much rules out visiting most places in the universe. But I still dream of travel, and in my own way, I still do it. No, honestly. Just the other night I went to Japan, London, Australia, somewhere in the desert, and round the corner to my friend Veronica's house. I had great big huge long conversations with millions of different people, and ran for a bus, and ate weird fruit that was all prickly and very very sweet, and got incredibly hot, and fell in love. And when I woke up I was absolutely exhausted. And quite surprised, because I was still in my own bed. I'd been travelling in my dreams.

Astral travel. It was really big in the 1970s, apparently. I mean, people have always done it, since time began, but they maybe didn't know until someone explained it to them. It's quite ancient and sacred. I discovered it because of a book I got from a jumble sale. It's written by a man called T Lobsang Rampa. He's actually a plumber, I think, living in New York, I think, but he says he's the reincarnation of a lama. And he wrote books about the third eye and attaining inner peace.

Anyway, I thought his book looked quite interesting so I bought it, took it home, sat in the kitchen and started reading it with a piece of carrot cake. Then the phone rang, so I went through to the living room to lie on the sofa and answer it, and it was this guy I've been sort of interested in. We call each other up and have long talks and it's good fun, but I don't know if he really likes me, or even, if he did, if I'd go out with him. It's a sort of casual flirtation style of relationship. So, anyway, there we were, chatting away like dafties, and he asked me – Ken, that's his name; he's got glasses – Ken asked me what I'd been doing, and I told him about the astral travel book, and how I thought I might try it. And he began to make all these jokes about not forgetting my toothbrush and wearing bed-socks in case it was cold wherever I was going, and keeping my passport in my pyjamas just in case. And I went 'ha ha ha, gosh, very funny, Ken'. But when we'd finished talking and I'd put the phone down I felt quite annoyed, I have to say. I didn't want to lose the glow, obviously, but there was a niggling feeling that his sarcasm had tipped some balance, and I didn't really like him that much, or, at least, I didn't respect him. I personally always think a person should open his mind before he opens his mouth.

Anyway, I finished the book in a flash, and I really enjoyed it. So I went out to look for more in charity shops, and over a few weeks I found quite a lot, not to mention some rather nice earrings – made of silver wire, like cobwebs, with wee red bits in the middle for the spiders – and a fab old green and yellow teapot, which I gave to my Gran. It was only £3.50 from Help the Aged – or as my Dad says 'Help! The Aged!'

So, the books; I read them all, and at night I lay in bed breathing deeply, in, out, in, out, the way he suggests, and tried to direct my thoughts and achieve total relaxation and drift off. The first few nights I got so relaxed I could hardly get up in the morning, and my Mum had to practically shout at me. And I didn't remember anything. But I kept at it, and eventually one night I found myself sort of awake in my sleep and – it's really hard to explain – floating on the ceiling. And I looked down and saw myself curled up in the bed, with my toes sticking out under the duvet, and my hair all over my face. I mean, I could really see it – I could identify the exact same nightie I was actually wearing, the one with the blue stripes and the polka dots on the pockets. I could even see the scars on my knees from when I fell off my tricycle when I was six. It was amazing!

After that it was just like learning to drive. I got used to it, sort of mentally changing gears and engaging the clutch and using the wing mirrors and stuff. And I began to travel all over the place. And one of the first things I did was meet up with Ken. We were in a bar, in the dream. Well, an astral projection of a bar, I suppose. He was leaning towards me, being quite flattering and affectionate, but I was pushing him away and saying 'No'. He tried to hold my hands and I was just going 'No, get off, sorry, not interested.' Uch, it was creepy. And when I woke up, I felt totally convinced that it had actually happened, the way you do sometimes, and I just did not want to see him or talk to him. Maybe he got the message, telepathically, because the next day I kept looking at the phone, like 'don't ring' – and it didn't.

It's funny, with all this astral travel I was doing, I found myself falling asleep during the day. I'd be on the sofa reading T Lobsang Rampa while watching *Bargain Hunt*, and just drift off, and go to Iceland or somewhere. The country, not the frozen food shop. When I woke up, all woozy, there'd be my Mum and Dad, looking down at me with a frown for drooling on the cushions. Actually, my Dad thought it was all a big laugh, and teased me rotten about it. 'Is that you off with that Tinned Lobsterama guy again, Marina?' he'd go.

My Mum didn't see it the same way, though. We very nearly fell out over it in actual fact, because she's quite devout. For instance, when she hears people on the telly criticising the Pope, her mouth goes in this wee thin line like Kenneth Branagh's and she dives into the kitchen and starts banging frying pans around. If she even sees a picture of Reverend Ian Paisley she starts muttering 'I'll give you the Irish question laddie . . . oh yes . . .' She has quite strong feelings about religion. Anyway, one evening when we'd been arguing a bit, me and Mum, about how many Gods there were and reincarnation and the Holy Ghost, I went to bed feeling quite irritable, and tossed and turned for ages and couldn't sleep. I put the light back on and sat up and read a few pages out of the new Michael Connelly novel that I'd got out of the library, and that must have done the trick, because the next thing I know I'm floating off into that same astral bar from before, and Ken's there, and we start talking, and it's weird, because all of a sudden I do really fancy him. He has gorgeous white teeth, and I keep looking at them, and then – God, this is really embarrassing – I kiss him. And he kisses me back, and I can feel his teeth against my tongue. Crikey, it went on forever. He had his arms round me, and I didn't object at all, but all the while I was thinking 'Well, Marina, are you just fickle, or what?' And I don't remember anything else, but the next morning when I woke up I couldn't stop blushing and smiling to myself like a big moon-face.

And guess what? About five minutes later, Ken phoned! I felt about eight years old again, stuttering and standing on one leg, and twisting the phone cord round my fingers, and laughing in that mental way. He asked me if I was still interested in travel, because he wanted me to go out with him for the day, and it was to be a surprise. I said yes, I was. He said he'd meet me at Central Station at 10.30 a.m., and I said should I bring anything, and he said no, just your wee self, Marina, and I'm telling you, I was practically having kittens.

I had a horrible ten-minute panic about what to wear – you know, sophisticated or casual, grunge or femme fatale. But it was cold and raining and only 9.45 a.m., so I just put on my newest jeans and a red shirt and my seude boots and a raincoat and my black hat, and took £10 and my signing-on card and a packet of Polo mints and rushed out the door. And then I rushed back in to leave a note for my Mum, and dump the hat and borrow her umbrella, and added a scarf, and rushed back out again and got the tube to the station. And Ken was there, where he'd said he'd be. My heart went *boing*, and *zippedee-doo-dah*, in a weird tribal dance, because he was wearing a red shirt too – it was like fate. Argh! The lap of the Gods, or what?

Anyway, we walked down the platform past the big London trains, and I thought where are we going? But in behind that there was a tiny wee one with only two coaches and we got on that and it chugged off. We sat across the table from each other and we talked, but only in that 'so, how are you, then?' sort of way, which you do when you're nervous. I was bursting to ask where we were going, but I didn't want to spoil it for Ken. I still felt all moony about him, because of the dream, and whenever he smiled, I ogled his teeth. When the train stopped, he made me close my eyes so I wouldn't get a clue, and after about ten minutes he said 'Right, this is it' and we got off, and left the station, and started walking up a pavement. And I began to recognise where we were. Ken looked at me then, so I made my face a blank when he asked 'Have you guessed yet?' and I went 'No.' But I had, I knew he'd taken me to Pollokshaws, and we must be heading for the Burrell Collection.

So, sure enough, that's where we spent the day. If you've never been, you have to imagine it as a bit like the place in that Orson Welles film, where at the end he's dreaming about his sledge. The man he played – Orson – Mr Kane – was incredibly rich, and his mansion was stuffed with amazing antiques from all over the world, including whole rooms from other people's houses, doors, stained glass windows, chairs, curtains, everything. The Burrell Collection isn't in a big echoey old castle like the Kane house, though; it's very modern, a really beautiful place, you feel as though you could step through the glass walls into the trees outside.

The stupid thing was, because I didn't want to disappoint him, I didn't let on to Ken that I'd been there before. I mean, I could see he was enjoying being the guide, the Man of the World who Knows Facts. Not telling him made me uncomfortable, though, and as the day went on I had to remind myself all the time – this is the guy you kissed, astrally, at least, and you enjoyed it, so stop being so critical. But his attitude bugged me. You know how professional types, like lawyers, always have to know everything and offer judgements? Even if you say you like tomato soup, they want to know why and what kind, and if you say Campbell's they'll make out a case for Heinz, and if you say well, yeah, but I still like Campbell's, they'll butt in and argue that there's no case for tinned soup whatsoever, kind of tying the whole subject up in red tape and throwing it in the filing cabinet, argument over. Well, Ken is a bit like that. He isn't a lawyer, but his Dad is, and his Mum's a teacher, and maybe that's the problem, because it wasn't my idea of a romantic day out, it was more like a sixth year study project.

After about three hours of it I felt like I'd really had enough. I was getting all rebellious, wanting to disagree with him, I don't know, sort of like Fletcher Christian and Captain Chay Bligh. We'd just got to the ceramics section, which is one of my favourite bits, where there are lots of beautiful ornamental teapots in the shape of frogs and lily pads and fruit and stuff, and you won't believe it but I saw one that was exactly like the one I'd bought for my Gran.

I was flabbergasted. I just sat down in front of the wee thing and gazed. Ken went droning on, pointing out some Japanese swords and telling me about samurai legend, like he was the only one who'd ever read *Shogun*, but none of it registered on me. I was too amazed. I scribbled down the details about the teapot on the back of my hand, so I could find out more later.

And suddenly, it all fell into place – astral travel, Ken's surprise, teapots – I knew it was all meant. Cosmically. Now I know what Richard Gere meant when he talked about epiphanies.

Eventually Ken realised I wasn't paying attention. He came up behind me and coughed and said it was probably time we were going, and I never told him about the teapot. I could tell that he felt I'd let him down by not being in awe of his brain; and I felt let down that he was not as exciting to be with in real life as he was in the other life. So we caught the train back, not talking much, and got into

Glasgow and stood there and both said 'Well, it's been fun, we must do this again some time, another museum perhaps' and so on, and then we sort of half-kissed, half-collided and bumped noses, and he went his way and I went mine. End of romance.

But not end of story. I went round to my Gran's the next again day and told her all about the teapot. And she said 'Well, pet, you have it back' and I said 'No, not at all' and she said 'No, no, I insist' and we hummed and hawed a wee bit but finally she said 'Look, Marina, take it to Christie's and get it valued'. So I did. And it wasn't the exact same teapot, it was a later copy, but still worth quite a lot, and it sold at auction two months later. I'm not telling you how much. I bought my Gran a brand new teapot (for £12.99 from House of Fraser) which she seems quite happy with. And I put the proceeds of the sale into my bank account, to save up for world travelling.

Because of T Lobsang Rampa I thought I might go to Nepal, or Egypt, or somewhere spiritual, you know? But then I remembered the mosquitoes. So maybe I'll go to New York instead. You never know, T Lobsang Rampa might still be there, and I could get his advice about life, and other worlds, and plumbing and everything. And then send all the facts to Ken on a postcard.

Skins

Close-up, it's an alien object, a magnified fly's eye. Pull focus a fraction and the thing changes, becomes mundane; black nylon tights stretched double-layered over a metal hoop, a pop-screen in front of a heavy-duty microphone. Widen the shot and there's a human face. A 45-year-old man with smooth, clear skin. An actor. As he leans in to the mic his eyes look down, his lips part, he breathes in, holds it, then, smoothly, his voice emerges in a warm, upbeat tone.

'Two four-hundred and twenty-five gramme packs of own-brand spaghetti for the price of one, just eighty-nine pence; three lunch-pack Hi-Juice one hundred and fifty millilitres, any flavour, ninety-nine pee; and family size jars of crinkle-cut fancy beetroot or cocktail gherkins, only sixty-nine pence each . . . what?'

The actor stops. The sound quality in his headphones has changed.

'Hey, have to stop you there, Jack.'

'Yeah?'

'Pee?'

'Oh. Sorry.'

'Yeah, we need to be consistent . . .'

'You'd prefer pence for all of them, yeah?'

'Yeah, pee's been vetoed by the client. Too down-market.' The producer's voice.

'And yet such a basic human function.'

Faint titters filter from the control room into Jack's ear canals.

'Okay . . . from the top, please . . .' says the sound engineer.

'Yup.'

Jack sits at a small baize-covered table, slightly hunched, with his hands resting palms-down on denim-clad thighs. He concentrates on a couple of sheets of paper, startlingly white under the glow of an anglepoise. Black type lies on the surface of his scripts like a team of synchronised ants awaiting the signal to start dancing. Beyond the immediate pool of light sit a water jug and glass, a pencil, his metallic specs case. Beyond that lies the shadowy depth of the studio. It's the ground floor of a converted chapel, walls panelled with grey egg-box style foam, sections hung with heavy slate-blue drapes to provide baffles, navy-blue carpet tiles on the floor and, high on the east wall, a tiny cobwebbed window. One quarter of the floor space is taken up by a full drum kit. Jack likes to think of it as his, he's played it often enough, but his serious muso days have been over for a while.

Under the table, Jack's feet are set neatly for balance, as though he might need to spring out of the chair. He wriggles his toes, bounces his legs, scratches his knee, shoogles his shoulders like Elvis, as the computer jumps back to start. For a few moments his face contorts in a slo-mo scream, flexing tense muscles until his jaws crack, then he yawns, rubs his eyes, and settles down to start his spiel again. 'Blah blah blah . . .' He reels it off precisely a couple of times with variations of emphasis on *just*, *only*, and *own-brand*. At the end of each take his chest hurts slightly, his lungs emptied of air. Too many words per second, too little space to breathe. But it's fine, they like takes 4 and 5, and now the sound engineer, Wilf, will compile a rough edit for the client to okay before they let him go, still within the booked hour. One eye on the clock, Jack shuffles his pages of script, removes the heavy padded headphones and slings them round his neck, leans back in the chair and stretches his arms up and out and down, arching his back, hearing his spine click.

Jack watches himself do all these things, his own private recording of every minute of every day, the director's cut. He's used to observing himself at work and play, used to being observed. The nature of the job is largely to be visible. Moments of downtime make him edgy, though. During breaks in filming, out on location, when he has a minute or an hour to resume his own state of mind, his shoulders drop forwards, mouth softens, eyes blink, he feels smaller, hears his voice alter pitch. Voice-overs are different. In this studio he's known and trusted and liked, he's a regular. He can turn up slouching, unshaven, grumpy, until Sheila upstairs has plied him with strong coffee, and they all know he'll deliver. This one, this job, it's for a new client, so he's tidied up a bit, made an effort to be friendly and funny. Not brown-nosing, just diplomacy, using the charm women often tell him he has, if he'd care to use it.

The studio is shabby. Wilf's spending more time these days nursing rock bands than courting advertising agencies, regressing to his old hippy-surfer persona. Inside the outsize sound booth doesn't much matter, it's only a temporary kennel for the actors, but through the large pane of glass which separates them Jack watches Wilf and the agency producer chatting and swivelling in their mismatched black and red typing chairs, sipping from commercial radio mugs, their faces pale under the 80s' style spotlights. Behind them are shelves stacked with CDs, an ugly wall clock with guitar hands, a sectional sofa covered in blaze-orange fabric, a couple of spindly plants, a bowl of green apples and another of brightly wrapped chocolate biscuits, and then the door to the murky corridor and the outside world. The glamorous biz of show, reduced to bare essentials. Bigger agencies prefer the blond wood and cafetière ambience of custom-built studios to this no-frills place, despite Wilf's expertise.

Though the 'phones are round his neck, Jack can hear the ongoing edit, the compressed, tinny noise of a jingle, the punchy listing of supermarket bargains in his own voice, the cheery tag line and end sting. Wilf confers with the producer briefly, then flicks a switch and says, 'You're done, mate, come on through.'

Collecting his jacket from the second chair, Jack tucks away his specs, clears his throat, and heads for the doors, his side of a pair of heavy soundproof panels which form an airtight seal between him and the control room. The sub-lock, he's heard Wilf call it. Visions of terrified, bearded submariners from *Das Boot* flit through Jack's mind every time he enters and exits, including now, as he spins the handle and pulls. Tugs on it. Tugs again. Seriously hauls at it.

'Aw, c'mon . . .'

He goes back to the table and taps the mic, but Wilf is turned away. Jack holds the headphones up to his ear, waits for him to turn back, then gestures at the door. Wilf looks puzzled, but toggles the talkback switch again, and Jack bends to the mic and enunciates, 'Aye, ha ha, there's just the tiny matter of the inexplicably locked door . . .'

'It's just stiff,' says Wilf.

'No . . . it's not just stiff, it's shut. You try it.'

Wilf moves out of vision, to try the door from his side. The producer adopts a tolerant smile, and props his mock-Prada loafers on the edge of the console. Jack can hear the faint squeak of the man's chair. Wilf comes back into view looking puzzled.

'God, Jack, sorry, man. This side's working but not the inner one. There's not even any give in the handle, that's really odd . . . never happened before . . . you didn't hear any funny noises when you closed it earlier?'

'Nuh. It was pretty stiff though, had to practically shoulder it.'

'Hang on, I'll try to get this sorted out.'

Jack sighs, and puts down his jacket. Wilf swivels to the phone.

'Hate to sound callous, Wilf, but I have to get this ad on air by four,' says the producer. He taps his watch, looks at the wall clock as if the watch-tapping wasn't clue enough. The talkback goes dead again. Through the looking glass, Wilf and the producer confer silently. Jack fumes a bit, and sighs. Finally, he gets a packet of fags out of his jacket, gestures rudely at the No Smoking sign, and lights up.

Wilf keys talkback.

'Jack, I'm going to dub this off as quickly as I can for Clive and I've got Sheila on the phone trying to get a joiner, so hang loose, okay?'

Jack says nothing, merely gives a smile that is not amused, blows smoke down his nose. He can see Wilf's dilemma. Clive? Wanker. Jack chucks his fag packet on the table, and ambles around the room, swishing a hand along the drapes. When this place was a chapel it might have held a congregation of sixty at most, tightly packed into their pews. Where once they'd have looked nominally heavenward at a high, vaulted ceiling, now there's a lower one, the upper floor of office space and Wilf's personal living quarters. At the back of the chapel there's an old door; it's supposed to be an emergency exit but no-one with a lot of instruments and electrical equipment wants a door that can be bust open by thieves, so it's never used. Jack tugs at the wrought iron ring handle, tries to force the painted-over bolts, looks for a key. Nothing. Black marks from Health and Safety, tut-tuts from the insurance guys, no doubt. He wanders back into the centre of the room, tips a handful of cigarette ash into his water glass and drops the butt in too. He sighs deeply, catches himself, breathes in slowly and exhales with control. It's not at all small for a studio space, but it's feeling smaller now.

Jack sits down at the drum kit, picks up the sticks and plays a very gentle tap-tap here and there. He's just footling, just passing the time, teasing the skins, because jammed doors don't present insurmountable obstacles and he's never been more than mildly claustrophobic. His hands like the heft of the drumsticks, and he can feel the muscles in his arms relearning the weight. He starts slow, finds the beat on bass drum, hi-hat and snare, then fills it out across the kit, a straight-ahead funk groove. In, as they say, the pocket.

Auditioning for bands in the past he'd never mention the acting, afraid of being labelled a poof, but when he auditioned for theatre work he'd made a point of it, showed up in a t-shirt with sleeves rolled to show his biceps. Female directors liked the look, liked the brawn with brain, while the men were usually intimidated by his physique. Once, in a rock-and-roll agit-prop company, touring all over the country, he'd had fan letters from women in the audience most nights, keen to buy him a drink. He'd see them in the pub after the show, they'd come up and smile and touch his arms, their eyes gliding from the prominent veins to the neatly manicured nails, impressed at such evident masculinity paired with careful grooming. They wanted to take him home, and he let them. He knows his hands are good, and his blue eyes and dark hair, a Celtic look from his father's side of the family.

Jack's father had no music in him, preferring gardening to other hobbies. Preferred it to people, really. As a kid, Jack would see his Dad bent over some bush with a pair of secateurs and wonder at those small, precise motions, that careful attention, evidence of some sort of passion, that didn't translate into his dealings with wife and child. A memory from being about five; dressed in a hand-knit sweater and shorts, little Jack ran round and round the rose bed banging on a saucepan with a spoon. His mother, invisible inside the kitchen, shouted at him to shut up, but his father continued to trim and tend his plants as if he were deaf. Mum came out, took away the pan and walloped Jack's behind with the spoon, three hard whacks. As he cried, his father looked up briefly and said, 'What's the matter?' His mother turned round and marched back to the house, calling over her shoulder, 'Dinner's on the table, there's no pudding. Come in now and wash your hands.' Deprived of his noise-makers, Jack trailed after her nervously, wondering if it was his fault about the pudding. Dad walked quietly behind him up the path, wiping sap off the secateurs with his handkerchief. Jack waited at the kitchen door in the hope that his father might go in with him, take the brunt of his mother's mood – from inside came the sound of cutlery being rattled with unnecessary force – but Dad just shooed him ahead. Jack moved swiftly past the sink, skirting the aproned figure, into the toilet, where he lathered his hands with oatmeal soap until the skin puckered. When he emerged his father was still outside, smoking a cigarette. Mum sat in her place at the table, saying nothing. By the time they'd all sat down to eat their lunch the potatoes were stone cold and the grey heaps of mince had congealed, showing white flakes of fat around the edges, like icy puddles on turned earth. At his father's funeral on a winter morning, the teenage Jack had looked at the dark soil under a light frost and immediately thought about mince and tatties.

Jack increases the tempo, tries to remember a tune to fit to it, but nothing comes, he's only thrashing, not playing. Still, he keeps at it, varying the patterns. Suddenly he's thinking about the Sex Pistols and the anger of their music, though punk was never his thing. Anger, though, yes, he's often felt that absolute rage, that desire to say 'Fuck you, I'll show you, you bastards.' He doesn't know why he began drumming, but he does remember his mother's disapproval.

'Why don't you do something with your qualifications? Why d'you have to make this stupid racket, and spend time with those people, drinkers and time-wasters the lot of them? D'you think this is what I wanted for you?' Her voice is right there in his head, always, his own personal instant replay. Maybe he needed to make the noise to drown her out, maybe he needs it even now. He pushes the pace, his muscles burning. Thrashes the bass, whacks the toms, hits the snare with a rimshot. More heft. H. E. F. T. Hit Every Fucking Thing. That's what he does, tunes out from his surroundings and hears only thunder until the sweat trickles down his back and his wrists ache.

The cymbals are still trembling when Jack gets up from

the drums. They resonate in a silvery whisper while he's putting down the sticks, hush into silence while he walks away to the table and repositions the chairs very gently and exactly. He lights another fag, his hands shaking. Then he walks over to the stuck door, hunkers down, feels the carpet. It's wet, like a piece of moss. He squints up, sees the slight staining on the ceiling where water has come in overnight and swollen the wood and the wool carpet. He straightens up, rummages in the gloom beneath the table, and finds a fan heater. He drags it as close as he can to the damp patch of carpet and turns it on full blast. He'd like someone else to admire his handywork, but when he peers into the bright glare of the control room, there's nobody there. The man with the leather coat will be on his way back to the agency already, and Wilf has other jobs to deal with, other clients to call, while he waits for a joiner.

Jack sits again at the baize-covered table. He hangs the headphones round his neck in case Wilf comes back, then puts them on properly to obliterate the rackety sound of the heater. He picks up one of the script pages, starts to fold it into different shapes, making himself one of those pointy pyramid things kids use for telling fortunes. He sticks his fingertips into it, and holds it up to his face. It looks like the beak of a bird, and he animates it, provides a voice for it, several voices. A Southern Baptist preacher, a Glasgow tough guy, Kermit the frog. He progresses to Ken Dodd, does Sean Connery, *of courshe* . . . tries Gielgud, segues to Brando. Brando with an edge, sulking. Brando as the Godfather, selling fancy-cut beetroot, Brando as Colonel Kurtz, opening a jar of gherkins. 'The horror. The *horror*.' Jack tires of the game, puts the paper puzzle aside and lets his mind drift. Where did he learn that paper trick? A TV programme? *Vision On? Blue Peter, Magpie, Crackerjack?*

'Jack?'

The sound comes shrilly through the 'phones. Wilf is back, peering at him through the plate glass like a kid at an aquarium. For a moment, Jack feels like a grouper stalked by Jacques Cousteau.

'Are you okay, mate?'

'Dandy.' Jack rubs his face.

'The joiner's going to be here in five . . . listen, d'you need me to call anyone? Agent, or whoever?'

'Nah. What's the time?'

'Just coming up to the hour.'

'Feels like several weeks.'

'Are you claustrophobic?'

'Well, I wasn't yesterday . . .'

'Be out in a jiff.'

'Tell him it's maybe the rain. Or your washing machine. You've got a bloody great leak in the ceiling . . . Wilf? Aw for fuck's sake.' He's gone again.

Jack removes the 'phones, folds his arms across the table and rests his head on them. Lying like this enhances the clamour of blood pounding through his body, thud, thud, as if it too wants to escape from confinement. He closes his eyes and tries to ignore it, but his attention is snagged by the tiny rasping of his shirtsleeves against the baize, scritch, scritch, scritch, with every change of breath. Metronomic, a slow beat like a death march. He wills himself still, tries to use the syncopation to steady his thoughts. Being silent and being left alone in the dark are two things he's always disliked, but has trained himself to endure. As a child he needed the bedroom door to be left ajar so that light from the street shining through a little window on the landing let him see the shape of his room. Waiting backstage for a gig, standing between folds of dark material in the wings of some theatre, listening for his cue, he would close his eyes and count off the seconds until he could no longer bear to be blind.

Jack remembers his first train journey to London, aged seventeen; the dusty golden brown moquette of the second class seats, the creak and rattle of the coaches and the strange metallic smell of the brakes, and those moments in tunnels when the brutal flood of electric light revealed his own face in the window, a pallid mask of apprehension. The journey back; tired, disappointed, feeling the effects of four cans of Carlsberg. Gazing out at black fields and distant flashes from cars passing on country roads miles away. Standing smoking in the corridor by the open window, where an older woman gave him the slow smile. Following her to the toilet and kissing her, lipstick smeared all over her chin, her skirt up around her hips, the noise of the train pressing on its tracks, urging them on until they were thrust into the darkness of another tunnel.

Heedful of a new sequence of sounds, vibrations travelling up his body from the floor, Jack gets up, leans across the table and presses his face to the glass. Far right he can see Wilf's back; he's watching as another man, the joiner, beavers away at the outside of his door. Jack goes up to his side, tries to help by turning the handle. He can feel the wood shudder under his hands, and his pulse speeds up at the thought of freedom. He steps back just in time to avoid being hit as the door opens a little, ripping the carpet in the process.

'Try not to totally break the fucking thing, it cost a

fortune,' mutters Wilf. The opening increases inch by inch, then the thick panel stops on rucked carpet, wedged again, but it's okay, it's just enough of a gap that Jack can squeeze his head, shoulders, hips through the opening and out out out out out.

'Jesus . . .' Jack reaches for the back of a chair, which spins under his hand.

'You okay there, pal? Take it easy, sit, sit. Want a coffee?'

'Eh? . . . Fuck . . . No, I'm fine. Just a cab . . . Nuh, actually, don't bother, I'm . . . going to . . . walk . . . Need to get out in the air . . .'

'You sure you're okay?'

Jack is speechless. He heads for the street door, passes Sheila at reception, lifts a hand in reply to her questioning look.

He bursts out into the street. The traffic noise blares in surround-sound. Breath roars loudly in his ears. He puts a hand out to the wall, feels dizzy, bends down to breathe better, legs apart, waiting for his heartbeat to normalise.

* * *

That night, Jack's dreams are particularly detailed. He finds himself in the house of his childhood. An ordinary 1950s' semi in a suburban section of a city, unremarkable except that it is his home, and he recognises it by the scent of furniture polish and the heavy thud of the front door as it swings shut behind him. He's in the hall. He knows there's a dark space under the stairs, closed in by wood panelling painted cream. The door catch on the outside is a simple piece of wood on a nail, easily turned to slip into an answering piece on the jamb. Now, Jack is in this, his favourite hidey-hole, listening to footsteps clack to and fro along the corridor, his mother's impatient pacing. She calls his name and he doesn't answer. Her gait quickens, clomp, clomp, in the direction of the kitchen, making a lighter sound on the lino, tick, tick, tick. Perhaps she's standing at the back door, looking for him out in the garden. Jack's perspective shifts, he floats up and follows to observe, hovers behind his mother, invisible, gauging the tension in her body, seeing the strong ankles in low-heeled court shoes, the black and white tweedy fabric of her coat, the gleam of her smartest patent-leather hand-bag dangling from one arm. Then she turns and once again he's under the stairs. A cavernous space for a small child, but he's scrunched up into one corner, perched on a bundle of newspapers, next to enamel buckets, empty bottles, and the extra coal scuttle. Why is he hiding?

Suddenly the door opens, light spills in and his mother's feet and legs fill the frame. Jack's looking up, trying to see her face, but he doesn't want to move. He's scared. Her coat flares out as she bends from the waist, the checked pattern swirling uncomfortably close, a bold fractal wave, and he closes his eyes. But her hand reaches in. The hand, foreshortened, swoops at him like an eagle's claw, with fingers sheathed in black suede, fingers growing longer and longer and longer. The hand wakes him, shakes him from sleep. He's gasping. He struggles out of the damp sheets and sits on the edge of the bed, swallowing back tears.

*   *   *

Jack visits his mother. He stands beside her bed, looking down at her shrunken shape under the covers. Blue-white hair falls in wisps across her brow, a once-tight perm extinguished by illness and medication. She's so still she might be dead. The bedside table with the covered water jug and plastic beaker contains no vases, no cards, no bottles of special invalid drinks. Jack's brought a small bunch of tulips and he places them just below her feet on the beige woven bedspread. Too late, he remembers that she never liked cut flowers except the roses his father grew with such care. Jack remembers the arrangement in the formal front room of that house, always the same green glass vase on the same cream crocheted doily, but the flowers ranged from brilliant yellows and blood reds to subtle peach and apricot tones. He'd inhale their scent as he did his homework at the dining table, sometimes looking up with a start when a tiny noise alerted him to the fall of a petal.

* * *

A week later, Jack is standing in his mother's kitchen. He's wearing a suit and dark tie. The room looks much the same forty years on, except for some stacked, empty cardboard boxes piled on the floor next to the back door. One box contains a couple of childhood annuals, an album of family photographs, a mantel clock decorated with cherubs under rubbed gilt, a pair of brass candlesticks, a wooden pencil case. Jack takes off his jacket, drapes it over a chair, then flicks on the radio by the sink for company while he works. He picks up a bundle of envelopes, finds a butter knife to open them with. The cards all read 'Get Well Soon' except for one in palest lilac, featuring a photograph of arum lilies and the words 'Thinking of you at this sad time'. He looks at each card, lines them up on the dresser against the yellow gingham-checked china. Then he picks them up again and folds them in half and half again, and looks around for the wastebin. It annoys him not to find it under the draining board where it used to be.

Jack walks out of the kitchen into the hallway, past the staircase with its polished banister, and stops. Under the staircase is the cupboard in which he hid as a child. Not a Wendy House, not a teepee, but a refuge. The paintwork on the door is chipped now. Gazing at it, Jack can't remember what brought him out of the kitchen. He's standing in a hallway watching himself stand in a hallway. The silence in the house offers no hints. Was he about to go upstairs?

He walks back into the kitchen, looks around vaguely at his jacket, at the boxes, the inexpensive radio, the clock above the door, the cheerful yellow dinner service. He looks at the crumpled wedge of cards in his hand, puts them down on the dresser. Again he walks out into the corridor, his boot heels clicking against the lino, clacking on the wood, and stops in front of the cupboard door. What is it he needs from here?

He opens the door catch and, as he squats down, a cool waft of damp paper and coal dust rises into his face, a zephyr of times past. The interior is empty except for a shiny red vacuum cleaner and several bundles of old newspapers. Leaning in to haul out a bale of the stuff, his face brushes against a gritty cobweb, and he recoils, teetering on his heels. The feeling of being half-in, half-out of the cupboard bothers him, and he hesitates, wondering what it might be like to curl up inside that space again, now so small and dark and smelling of corruption. What it might be like to be both inside and outside, watching himself walk around the empty house, hearing his own tread on the stair above. For a second he closes his eyes and imagines it, sees himself crouched in the dark, senses the damp of the newspaper under his bare legs, sees the door open and a black gloved hand reach in, catch his sleeve and pull him out. Feels the slap on the side of his face, the grip on his collar as he's marched into the toilet to wash his hands and knees. Hears his mother's voice. 'What am I to do with you? Stupid, annoying little boy.' The floury smell of oatmeal soap mixed with the warm perfume of his mother's coat, a cold flannel wiping tears off his flushed face. Trotting out to the drive, his mother's hand in his, the softness of suede.

Jack twists the wooden catch to close up the cupboard. He returns to the kitchen and drops the bound papers onto a chair. He rolls up the sleeves of his crisp white shirt, pulls out the cutlery drawer, rummages for scissors. He finds a bread knife, and saws at the heavy twine until it curls and springs apart. He lifts a faded copy of the *Courier* – circa 1981 – and unfolds it over the kitchen table. Opening one of the wall cabinets, he takes down a stack of un-matching dinner plates, odd coffee cups, a pink and white tureen, and his mother's favourite green glass vase. He sets them on the floor, on chairs or on the sideboard, and begins to wrap them individually in newspaper. The old ink transfers to his hands and each cup receives a grimy set of his finger-prints, a personal seal of dismissal. He's careful, but only enough to get the objects from there to the charity shops. One by one the pieces go into boxes, and he folds the card-board corners over and under each other, like rudimentary origami. Behind the crackle of newsprint and the clink of ceramic, he's aware of a rhythm, a beat, a tune, from the radio by the sink. The jingle of a radio commercial, and his own voice, stressing *just, only,* and *own-brand,* warm and professional and upbeat. Jack doesn't look up from his task.

French Lessons

FRANCE, SUMMER 1973

'*Pauvre bagnole*,' we crooned, 'poor car', urging our bottle-green Deux Chevaux over the bumps by leaning forward, patting the shabby plastic dashboard. Wisps of grass brushed the belly of the car, seed heads popping like corn through the rusted door-sill. Perhaps a hundred vehicles were already parked in the field, but few had floor-level air conditioning like ours. Mum applied the handbrake, got out and pretended to lock the damaged driver's door.

'Can I leave my jacket here?' Annie was proud of the budding breasts beneath her tie-dye t-shirt, and wanted the world to know it.

'No, darling, it'll get chilly later on, tie it round your middle if you don't want to wear it now. Come on, Trish. *Liliane, tu es venu devant?*'

'*Déjà*,' I corrected quietly, 'before, not in front of.' My schoolfriend Liliane smiled, and nodded, linking her arm with mine. I smiled back, and we joined the general drift of people crossing the fields towards the *fête*.

The *Fête Champêtre* at Croquelardit took place on the outskirts of a village near Agen, in the Lot Valley. Over four nights in midsummer, hundreds of people congregated in a large, walled park, set amongst orchards and small farms, to meet friends and dance, to drink and argue, and to celebrate before the hard work of harvest. Here, in autumn, swarms of wasps and fruit pickers vied for the juiciest nectarines and peaches, wiry men with bowed backs culled melons and pumpkins and, after the first frosts, a dawn patrol of field workers plucked the amethyst Santa Claras from the hard ground beneath their parent trees, sorted and boxed them, before the sun was high enough to rot them where they had fallen. Now, the fruit was still young and green as a teenager, and the only colours in the trees were from the gaudy strings of lights strung around the *fête*, illuminating the stalls and busy food concessions.

Ambling through the main gates we were met with an enthusiastic *'Bonsoir Mesdames!'* A dark and handsome semi-stranger took my mother's hand, kissed it, and placed it on his arm. She laughed, surprised, perhaps embarrassed, at his attentions but, when he insisted, she accepted his offer of white wine and oysters, *'pour la santé de maman'*, though she claimed to be too old to feel rejuvenated by shellfish, miming where words eluded her rather erratic vocabulary. With exaggerated courtesy, and grand gestures, our friend Ali seated us around a wobbly table and drinks were ordered.

We knew Ali slightly, through Liliane. He was thirty-ish, slim, fine-boned, with an almost aristocratic face, marred only by pockmarked skin and a broken nose. He wore his white jacket draped around his shoulders and adorned his neck with numerous gold chains, 70s' Las Vegas style. He worked as a guide and translator, his office the more tourist-frequented cafés, as well as the Algerian men-only bars – a crossover achieved by few, and in his case only by virtue of being a white-collar worker in a town dominated by a sprawling car-parts factory. Amongst the multiracial workforce, the palest-skinned newcomers, Poles, Italians, and Spaniards, looked down on the Algerians. Ali was elated to find a respectable British matron willing to acknowledge his charm and his intellect, and made great efforts to prove his intentions honourable.

'A toast – never forget your mother,' Ali commanded, gesturing with his oyster shell. 'You must honour her, she is sacred. Promise this!' Mum raised an eyebrow, and laughed, unconsciously smoothing her home-cut hair at the nape, while we all solemnly promised. Abba's 'Waterloo' blaring from several directions forced us to shout and enunciate operatically. Ali moved closer to Mum, and started to recount a story about Berber customs of hospitality. Annie sucked *menthe à l'eau* through her straw, Liliane sat straight-backed on her rickety chair, smiling rather ambiguously. I raised my glass of beer with grenadine syrup, scanned, tracked, noted. I was exhilarated and at the same time apprehensive of this unfamiliar contact with so much noise, so many people. Apart from school, and grocery shopping, we rarely went anywhere *en famille*, and scarcely socialised. Liliane was one of my few friends at school, and it had been her idea to come here. Local *fêtes* usually offered a simple *Bal Accordéon*, with plenty of smoochy dancing – '*Tu veux danser un slow?*' – for young and old alike, and we were used to seeing our elderly neighbours waltzing with concentration round the local bandstand, but here, at Croquelardit, French rock stars like Johnny Hallyday and Serge Llama were due to appear. They meant little enough to me, weaned on the distant gods of Johnny Winter and Bowie, but it was really the big time for Agen.

Around us the crowds ebbed and flowed. Families moved from stall to stall, little children eating candy-floss and ice cream, eyes unblinking, their parents constantly repeating, *'Non chérie, c'est trop cher'*. Groups of single boys and girls, feigning disinterest, passed each other by, tossing cigarette ends at feet like gloves in some ritual challenge. The atmosphere seemed tense, hormonally charged.

I narrowed my eyes till they were unfocused, seeing a kaleidoscope of colours and patterns in the mass of bodies – whites, pinks, blue and every shade of skin from Anglo-Saxon to darkest African – and wished I could paint. The abstract pattern of forms in motion induced a sensation which tugged at my stomach muscles like seasickness.

Liliane put her mouth to my ear and murmured that we should be exploring the rest of the *fête* so, permission granted and small funds secured, we drifted off, grudgingly taking Annie with us, leaving Mum and Ali to their purely linguistic flirtation.

As soon as we were out of sight, Liliane dug out a pack of Camels and lit up. Cigarettes, even unlit, were her props. At sixteen, she was a year older than me and already physically mature, small and slender with café-crème skin and masses of woolly black hair, from which came her nickname, Mouton. Her breasts were large, firm domes. She was never able to sit one out at dances as the entire male population attempted to discover whether she was padded or underwired. She complained about it, but only to me.

I tried to emulate her cool, though her ability to abandon responsibility for herself, particularly when she drank, was a factor I had come to recognise and worry about. Even now, on a single glass of pissy beer, Liliane swung her hips like a summons to prayer. I looked over my shoulder; yes, we already had a following, four young men, swaggering, smirking a little. Liliane knew without having to turn her head. As usual, a sense of warm confusion suffused me, a mental blush; irritation, a dislike of being examined and judged, but conflicting with that, a definite wish to be of romantic interest.

We linked arms and wheeled round into the Hall of Mirrors, a shabby tent in which perhaps a dozen convex and concave panels were lined up, the usual thing, but, in our heightened state, hilarious. Our slim legs, encased in baggy trousers, ballooned and shrivelled, our faces puffed and split in two when we laughed. Annie stood sideways, focused on her juvenile breasts expanding and contracting as she flexed her knees. Beside Liliane's shimmering hourglass shape, I watched my own torso swell like a time-lapse pregnancy under my favourite pink cheesecloth smock. When we tired of the mirrors, we gawped at the Leopard Woman, snarling from the gloom of her cage, shot at tin rabbits with pop-guns, threw hoops to win a hideous doll with violet eyes which we christened 'Leez' Taylor and allowed Annie to adopt, and checked out the pseudo-rock band, warming up the crowds for Johnny Hallyday's set. When we bought hot-dogs smothered in ketchup Liliane had a fit of giggles about the phallic symbolism, which was not missed by the male fan club, though they still kept their distance.

We returned to sit for a while with Mum and Ali. Annie was tired now, fidgety, feeling left out. Liliane's smile seemed glazed, her eyes fixed, but she ignored my warning look and accepted Ali's offer of another beer. She sipped, looking over Ali's shoulder to where the fan club loitered, smoking casually, flicking occasional glances our way. One of the men was half Vietnamese, with long, glossy hair and tight black trousers, and the more he looked at Liliane the more I wanted him to look at me. His companions were less exotic in their blue jeans and white shirts, but more arrogantly French Male.

Conscious of their admiration but never openly returning their interest, Liliane registered her contentment through narrowed eyes, like a sleek, contented cat.

What was she thinking? For all our camaraderie, I never really knew Liliane, never actually communicated to her anything I cared about. For me, books were more real and vital than anything else, whereas she had never read for pleasure, and probably never would. We had a shallow friendship, speaking in jargon and clichés which imposed on us a standard of behaviour at odds with our ages. At her prompting, I teased and rebuffed men, and made sexual jokes which I lacked the experience to comprehend. My informal education consisted of knowing looks, and haughty dismissal, which I practised daily on the acned *lycée* boys who sat astride their *vélos* at the school gates during break. When I could not understand their replies, I answered with a mimic's skill, using a phrase or gesture in which their piti-ful lust was made explicit. Outside the classroom, I was learning fast and acquiring excellent camouflage.

Ali took his leave, graciously, and Mum decided it was time to go home. Liliane didn't want to leave; she said we'd be sure to get a lift in an hour or so with her brothers. Mum accepted her suggestion without protest. Annie whined about being treated like a baby, but was yawning too hard to make much of an argument. Mum kissed our cheeks. 'Have fun, and don't be too late,' she said, and to Liliane something about looking after me which I knew even then to be an unlikely role for her. We made reassur-ing noises, and waved them off, Liliane with obvious relief.

Like jackals picking out stragglers, within minutes of my mother and sister departing, the pack circled and moved in. I've no idea now what all their names were, silly names probably, like Dédé or Toto, and I can only remember three of them in any detail: the Asian, to whom I was drawn aesthetically; a small, fast-talking, sharp-featured guy whom I immediately thought of as the Rodent; and the third, tall and fair, with thick curly hair, a rose tattoo on his left wrist, and a superior manner. They talked and joked and postured, like the guys from *Grease* but meaner. Liliane was in her element.

I wasn't ignored. My fair skin and blonde hair were unusual enough to draw comment in most situations. My accent allowed me to pass as French or Belgian, rather than English, and I cultivated that assumption, a subtle lie which deflected some of the sexual fervour of would-be Lotharios, the French fetish about English girls being equivalent to the English one about French girls. Trying to explain that I was, in any case, Scottish somehow made me seem more of a collector's item, so I played it down.

The Rodent nudged me in the ribs.

'So which of us do you want to go with?'

'What for?'

He winked at his friends. 'Well, for a little walk.'

Tattoo took me by the arm. 'I'll show you round, come on.'

I looked at Liliane. The men were still talking, but between us there was static. She would not meet my eye. Tattoo tugged at my arm and we were separating from the others, walking quite fast towards one end of the *fête*'s boundary walls.

My memory is of the blur of colour and sound as we passed stalls and people, all rushing by in the other direction, like figures on a merry-go-round, the sudden smell of grilling *merguez*, the perfume of night-scented plants, as we left the enclosure and walked into the darker fields beyond. Our feet rustled through long grasses. His hand on my arm was firm, the sensation quite pleasant, as long as I didn't look at him, didn't think about the passivity of being selected. Should I ask his name? Should I volunteer mine? What was the procedure for taking a walk with a total stranger? I ventured a simple question.

'Where are we going?'

'Not far.'

We cut past the car park field and headed towards some scattered houses, their shutters closed tight, impossible to tell if they were inhabited or abandoned. Tattoo stopped to look around, then pushed through a bit of broken fence into the overgrown garden of a house. Having a piss, I thought, and on impulse looked back – the *fête* seemed distant, miniaturised against the glowing sky, the music faint and crude – then he caught my wrist and pulled me through the fence. I half expected him to say 'Quick, hide, or they'll find us', as though we were kids playing some thrilling game of hide and seek, adventuring in a mysterious forest. Fairy tales and romantic novels formed the template for my imaginings, but not for his.

He lay on the ground, tugging me down beside him, then leaned over me, leaning on one elbow as I waited, in nervous expectation, for my first kiss. Instead he took my wrist and placed my hand over his groin.

'Touch it.'

'What?'

'Touch it. Pull down the zip.'

His tone was matter of fact. I wondered blankly what 'it' was. A curious lump in his jeans. He kept his hand tight on my wrist as I lowered the zip, moved my hand to press down against his underwear, and the warm, rigid object beneath.

I suddenly thought of my brother in the bathroom, when

I'd spied on him through the keyhole and seen him undress, the strange, wrinkly, dangling object which was my only previous sighting of male sexual equipment.

'Hold it.'

'What? No, I don't know how . . .'

'Just put your hand round it. Now move up and down – not so hard! Yeah, like that.'

Mechanically, I pumped. It seemed a pretty dull experience. After a while my hand got tired and my wrist hurt from being gripped and I stopped.

'No, you have to go on till I tell you to stop.'

'But I don't want to . . .'

'Do you want to get hurt?'

With his other hand he produced something from a pocket in his jeans, which clicked; he moved it closer to my face, so that I could see it, a knife, the blade as long as his fingers, a flash of silver in the moonlight. My fingers crept back to his penis, picked it up, and started rubbing, slowly, then faster. The rest of his body seemed to be in pain, legs twitching, neck jerking, as I jerked.

'*Suce moi* . . .'

My heart thudded in my ribcage.

Suck me. It was a plea. But for the knife, I could have been moved by that momentary reversal of power. Instead I felt revulsion. I remember the sound of my voice, cold and wavering.

'No.'

'You've got to.'

'No!'

'It's what the French girls do!' He sounded indignant.

'I don't want to, and I'm not French – let me go!'

'Stop shouting – do it, or I'm going to hurt you . . .'

'*No*! Let me go . . .'

He must have dropped the knife because he held both my wrists in his hands and was turned towards me, while I was on my knees pulling back against his grip. Behind us a house shutter groaned open, slapping against a wall, and a man shouted, 'Hey, people are trying to sleep in here! Go somewhere else, *nom de Dieu!*' I saw him, haloed in the lamplight, an elderly man in an old-fashioned nightshirt. As if trying to prove nothing untoward had been happening Tattoo let go of me and shouted back, '*Oui, bon, ça va*, okay,' and under his breath '*vieux connard*'. Old fool.

I got to my feet and started wading through the waist-high grass. After a few steps Tattoo caught up with me. We didn't speak. Every so often he'd try to take my arm but I shrugged him off and kept going, back to the lights and the crowds. Somehow everything looked the same, as though we'd never left, that couple still arguing, this couple still eating crêpes. Normality, except that in our brief absence the place had become filled with lovers. Tattoo put his arm firmly round my shoulders, slowing my pace. It felt strange, but everyone else was doing it, and the gesture offered an illusion of harmony and belonging, so this time I didn't struggle.

Liliane stood by the exit drinking from a bottle of Stella. She was smiling slightly, a meaningless expression given the alcohol, and shrugging as the Rodent whispered into her ear. It seemed to me that they hadn't moved, and that he'd got nothing from the evening's transactions. His eyes flicked from me to Tattoo and back a few times, and he grinned.

'Come on, we'll take you home.'

I looked at Liliane.

'No, it's okay, we've got a lift arranged with her brothers.'

'Hey, come on, don't be unfriendly. We're going your way, we'll take you.'

He drew Tattoo aside for a moment and whispered to him, and I hissed at Liliane, 'What are we going to do?'

Another feline smile. Liliane was going to do nothing. I didn't know if her brothers were there or not, didn't know how else we would get home. I couldn't leave her, and she wasn't going to be any help to herself or to me. I turned to look back into the *fête*, hoping to see my mother still there, someone, anyone I knew – and there was Ali, talking with an older man. I shouted, 'Hey, Ali!' and waved, but the noise of the *fête* drowned out my timid teenage voice, and he didn't look round. The Rodent was suddenly back at my side, his raised eyebrow questioning my action.

I explained. 'Oh, he's someone I know . . .'

'You know him? Christ, you want to stay clear of guys like that. Bloody Arabs! They fuck goats, dirty bastards. Hey, are we going or not? Come on!'

Liliane and I endured a cramped journey in the back of their little Renault van, squatting on the edge of a spare tyre amidst a clutter of plumber's tools, being driven round bends in some country road that I couldn't identify. Did we talk? I think I muttered something to Liliane about getting out as soon as we got to a village. In the front, the two men spoke so quietly and so quickly that I couldn't catch any words that made sense. Liliane seemed on the verge of falling asleep, and when I prodded her with an elbow she produced a little moan, like a child woken from dreaming.

After what might have been twenty minutes, the van turned off the tarmac onto gravel for a few hundred yards and halted outside a building. The men got out of the front cab, the Rodent crunching round to open the van doors.

Behind his head, the sky had changed from clear to dark and cloudy.

'Out you come. It's my brother's place – we'll go in, get a cup of coffee . . .'

'No thanks, we'll just stay here . . .'

'Oh come on, it's cold out here. Come inside.'

We followed them into the house. It was dark, unoccupied, but warm from the big enamelled kitchen stove. A large table and half a dozen rush-seated chairs were placed erratically in the middle of the space. Tattoo turned on a lamp and opened a door into another room.

'The WC is through here, if you want it?'

Tottering a little on her platform sandals, Liliane followed him through the door and he closed it gently behind them. Her absence made the room seem unaccountably claustrophobic.

'So, where's your brother?'

'He'll be here soon. Sit down – no, over here, it's warmer near the stove.'

I moved a few feet closer to the warmth but remained standing, arms folded about me. I avoided his gaze. I'd once been told I had honest eyes, and I didn't want to show my contempt, or my fear. He asked me a few questions – 'Where do you live?' 'What's your name?' I just shrugged, feeling foolish, but unwilling to be civil. He sighed, then with a jerk of his head to indicate Tattoo in the other room, he said: '*Il m'a dit que t'es bonne suceuse.*'

I thought first of licking ice-lollies on a hot day. Then I realised the implication, wanted to laugh, shout, throw a tantrum, swear on something sacred that it was a lie. Being told to do it at knifepoint was bad enough, to be misrepresented as having expertise was ominous.

'That's not true, nothing happened!'

'Don't be bashful. He said you were really good. Want to show me now? Come on.'

I shook my head, too angry to speak. Denial was futile, there was nothing to be said to this man which he wouldn't use to trap me. He walked towards me. From the other room, I suddenly heard Liliane's plaintive whine – '*Laisse-moi* – leave me alone!'

And then all the fury I had been unable to feel or express for myself came to me in her defence, superseding fear. I made a dash for the door, but the Rodent was there ahead of me.

'Is this fun? You want to be chased, *ma petite suceuse*? Or d'you want to sit on my lap?' His eyes were very bright, the way a dog's eyes are, when it waits for you to throw another stick. I could hear his breathing, fast, and my own, faster.

We faced each other across the broad kitchen table; my back was to the front door, and the door from behind which Liliane was moaning, now loudly and rhythmically, was equidistant between us. I could have tried to escape on my own, but it must have been obvious to him that I wouldn't leave without my friend, and he was very confident of eventual success. I tried edging closer to the door, only to be forced into retreat as he advanced. We danced this sequence a few times, and after a while Liliane stopped moaning. Her silence made the situation seem worse. Next time he moved I waited till he'd almost reached me, then tipped over a chair, ran to the bedroom door and hammered my fist on it, once, shouting – 'Liliane, get out here now!' – then was off again, back to the horrible merry-go-round of pursuit and escape.

Then everything seemed to happen very quickly, and in slow motion. Liliane pulled open the door and stepped into the kitchen; the Rodent came round the table just as she passed behind me, and instead of running from him I stood still, arms outstretched as if preparing to push him away. I yelled 'Get lost you bastard!' and perhaps he found me ridiculous and was so sure of himself, of my inability to fight back effectively against his will, his desire, his strength, expecting only some puny blows that, when I kicked him in the groin, it surprised him. It surprised me, the oldest trick in the book, and it worked. Then he was down on the floor, and I felt the cool rush of air behind me as Liliane opened the farmhouse door, and we fled.

Hand in hand we ran down the gravel track and onto the road, turning right, back the way we'd come in the van. We hadn't the breath to speak. I glanced at Liliane once – she was holding up her trousers with her left hand, her shirt was held by a single button near the waist and her breasts surged like matched racehorses. I wondered how she would explain to her mother the loss of her best bra. My throat ached from running with my mouth open. I kept looking over my shoulder, expecting to see the van's lights at any moment, sure they wouldn't let us go. Sure enough, within a few minutes I heard an engine and dragged Liliane off the road into the ditch. There was barely cover for a rabbit, but we cowered there together, half praying, half crying, until the car went by – an innocent old Citroën DS.

We lay in the ditch a while to get our strength back. When the night sounds became louder than our breathing, Liliane sat up, brushing dirt from her hands. She looked at me briefly.

'You know, if we reported them they could go to prison, because you're under age.'

Her careful reasoning impressed me.

Liliane grumbled at the damage to her clothing, but volunteered nothing of her recent experience and asked nothing of my mine. She fumbled with her zip, and did up what buttons Tattoo had left her. Neither of us had a watch, or much sense of the time, let alone direction, so we decided just to keep going up the road in the hope that we'd reach the *fête* again, and somehow get a lift. Twice more in about as many miles we had to jump behind bushes, but after a shuddering milk truck and a smart new Deux Chevaux had passed we began to feel safe, and talked about thumbing a lift. The next car, we agreed. Some ten minutes later we heard one noisily climbing the slope behind us, and we turned into its headlight beams, hands out.

The car slowed at some distance and then rolled gently forward to a stop beside us. Liliane peered into the passenger window, asking where they were headed. I could see nothing of the faces inside the car, though there appeared to be four people. I tugged at Liliane's arm. She said, 'Its okay, they're going near your house.' She smiled at me, and opened the front passenger door, indicating that I should ride in the back. Although every instinct told me it was a mistake, that I'd be safer sleeping in a field or hiding in a barn, my allegiance to Liliane was too strong to prevent me from following, and the moment for protest was gone.

As soon as I got in I realised all the passengers were men, and Algerian. There was some discussion going on, and a lot of laughter, and the two men in the front craned their necks round to look at me. They seemed to find the sight of me in their car hilarious. I didn't trust their smiles, their laughter. I looked away, down at my hands, out of the window. Then the car lurched off, and I was pressed up against the warm, bony shoulder and thigh of the man next to me.

The moon was hidden now, and only the headlights, as we swung through curves on the road, illuminated our progress past fields, the occasional shuttered house, slope-shouldered barns. An army of fruit trees fanning out ahead told me we were nearing Croquelardit. The road was empty, and I guessed it was late, perhaps 2 a.m. Guilt added itself to apprehension and exhaustion, as I pictured my mother waiting at home, seated at the kitchen table in her dressing gown, sipping tea, smoking, one eye on the clock, alert to every night sound, the dog sighing in his sleep an echo of her worries.

The noise of the engine was loud enough to obliterate most of our hosts' conversation, which was mainly in Arabic. When my neighbour turned and spoke to me in French, I had to ask him to repeat it, and watch his lips to be sure of understanding him.

'Are you not scared?'

'No.' The response was automatic, if untrue, but it seemed the only safe thing to say.

'You are not frightened to be in a car with four Arabs?'

'No.' If he wanted me to be, I wasn't going to give him the pleasure.

He grinned, bad teeth showing under a ragged moustache. The man beside him leaned over. His face was delicate, with the soft liquid eyes of a Labrador.

'It's not safe. You are too young to be out at night, you should be with a man. Don't you have brothers?'

'Yes. One. But he's in Scotland.'

'Ah, Scotland. Where is this?'

'It's in Great Britain – England? It's much colder there. We have a lot of snow.'

'Ah. Snow, yes, I have seen snow. And your brother, what does he do there?'

I hesitated an instant – if I told them he was at university studying fine art then the common ground we'd reached over the snow was going to vanish.

'He works in a factory. A factory that makes biscuits. He puts the jam into the biscuits.'

They didn't laugh. It had been one of Alan's best stories, working on the jam belt at Burton's Biscuits last summer in his university vacation, but to these men it was a real job, though not as tough as their own. I guessed they worked in the car-parts factory, but I asked anyway – they all did. I had passed the place often, a huge, grey, high-walled complex of buildings, a compound a mile long. The Algerian workers lived in tiny single-room prefab shacks on a piece of ground just across the road from the factory gates, breathing in its metallic dust day and night.

'Have you worked there long?' I asked. 'Is it bad?' The soft-eyed man replied, 'Two years. It's okay, but my family cannot join me. There is no room, even if I could get papers. I must work another two, three years, then I can tell my wife to come, and my sons.' He produced a photo, and in the dim light of a village street lamp I could make out two small boys standing in front of some shrubbery, squinting in strong sunlight. He told me their names. The atmosphere in the car seemed to change, as though someone had opened a window. Perhaps I had.

In the front, Liliane accepted a cigarette and talked quite happily with the driver. I thought I heard her mention Ali, saw the men nodding their heads. I asked more questions. Two of the men were married, with families thousands of miles away, and the other two despaired of finding love in this country; the French hated and mistrusted them, and girls would not talk to them. I thought of Tattoo and the Rodent; presumptuous, arrogant, colonialist.

'You are still not scared?' My neighbour scowled, trying to look ferocious.

I smiled at him. 'No.' It was true, now. I felt almost relaxed.

We reached the outskirts of town, and the first rows of workers' huts appeared on the left as the road straightened out, running alongside the factory. I'd heard men call the place Colditz, and it looked the part, grim and eerie in the floodlighting which enabled its constant operation.

Liliane shifted round to look at me. 'They have to go to work soon, shall we get out here and walk the rest?'

Hadn't she had enough? It was a further three miles to the village where I lived. After all the events of the night, the comfort of the car was too much to give up, the safety of companionship so longed for, that I shook my head, emphatic for once with Liliane, whose appetite for risk seemed boundless.

'Ask if he'll take us nearer the house.'

Our driver gave a great laugh. 'You sure you don't want to go to Scotland? Okay, I'll take you. Bad luck to walk this road at night, you could get picked up by filthy Arabs, eh?'

They dropped us discreetly just short of the village, by the old communal wash-house, where we shook their hands and watched as they turned the car in the square and drove away. Then we walked shivering through the mist towards home.

Olympia

I was six weeks old, eyes newly opened and blue as the sky, when my mother carried me the four storeys from basement to attic in her mouth. I hung docile in her grip, dreaming of nothing, until she dropped me on the upper landing behind some heavy curtains with a warning to be silent. But I was the oldest of five, bold and unthinking. Was I born to hide from experience? The old velvet was full of dust, and pushing against it provoked a violent fit of sneezing; suddenly alone, the noise of my tiny explosions terrified me! I opened my mouth to cry but was distracted.

Footsteps pounded on the steps as a young boy hurried breathless to the top. His enormous feet swept past my nose, he knocked at a door, and went quickly into a bright space, longer than it was broad, flooded with radiance from above. As he set down a heavy wooden case his coat stirred the floor, and dust motes, large as moths, danced in a shaft of sunlight. I was captivated. Racing forward to seize them, I tipped forward, rolled over and got up again, and sneezed once more, scaring myself into a shrill cry of fear. A second figure came forward and bent low to inspect me. His moustaches and beard were red-gold where the light touched them, like my mother's pelt.

'What's this,' he said, 'A little spy?' He held me in the palm of his hand, and I showed him my teeth in a yawn, at which he showed me his in a laugh. He put me down in a dark place by the door, but I came running back to the sunlight, suddenly confident, and pounced at his feet. 'You appoint yourself my shadow, then? Look, Pierre, this *mouchard* is black as an African, but under the light of the sun it is not a solid colour, unlike your sooty mixtures.' Pierre merely said, 'Yes, Monsieur, will Monsieur require a quantity of the Ivory Black this time?' Monsieur laughed: 'Yes, and plenty, for how else to paint the world in truth?'

Ah! The painful creak of hinges as Pierre opened his case to withdraw bottles of oil, their clink on the marbled surface of the table, the thud of heavy packets of pigment, the recital of colours – Viridian, Vermilion, Cobalt, Ultramarine – these sounds were to be the refrain of my nursery days, the song of my prime, the lullaby of my old age. Even now, the stench of linseed oil recalls for me the Rue de la Victoire, and my clumsy arrival at the studio of Edouard Manet.

My apprenticeship was rapid. I learned to keep to the shadows when strangers came in their tall silk hats with pocket watches and waistcoat buttons gleaming. At night I chased mice out of cupboards, defending costumes and props, and on quiet, sunny days, I would lie beneath Monsieur Manet's armchair to keep an eye on the darting activities of his loaded brush. At times he waved his arm, jabbed with it, scrubbed, pushed, pecked, like a bird reaching for insects; at other times he was content to glide or dab. Three paces back, three forward, repeated a hundred times a day. The scuffing sounds of bristle on canvas, the tink-tink-tink of brush ferrules against glass jars. His hands rubbed at his linen smock, plucked at his hair, scraped back the paint with his flat knife. He accompanied himself with a little humming or an exasperated exclamation when he was alone, but in company he became an expansive host, dressed always in fashionable cloth and with a cravat of some festive colour; confident, charming, a man with many friends. In their presence, I pretended indifference to the human circus, and would lie curled upon a leather trunk with my paws tucked under and eyes half closed, watching the play of light and shade across the Turkey carpet as visitors moved about the room.

Mademoiselle Victorine was my favourite, then, as she was his. Victorine Meurent, his model. 'Scarcely more than a kitten herself, but already a woman of character!' as Monsieur described her to the friend of his schooldays, Monsieur Proust. Victorine first came to pose one afternoon in a grey dress and cape, the veil on her hat pearled with moisture from the fog, and insisted on playing a funny little song on her guitar before she would settle into position. Monsieur drew many sketches, full-face and semi-profile, and afterwards he marched to and fro with them in his hands, very excited. On her next visit Monsieur asked her to wear a white blouse, and to sit half in shade, half in light, and look him straight in the eye.

'I wish your skin to be flooded with light, Mademoiselle,' said my master.

'Like this, Monsieur?' she asked, turning her head, and then sat serene and pensive for two hours, scarcely blinking. After that she came often. For weeks she posed as a bullfighter with a Spanish hat and sword, and tassels at the knees of her britches; another time with her guitar, in her own grey dress and coat, and a bunch of cherries held to her lips. Although she behaved with professional decorum in the pose, while she changed behind the screen she would tease me with a piece of silk or a fluttering handkerchief, until I'd pretend to grow infuriated and stalk off to my observation post. Contrite, she would soothe me on her lap until I purred, only to tease me all over again. It was a game from which we both took immense satisfaction.

She was clever, Victorine, with a spirit of independence. Her father was a patinator of bronzes, and she herself had modelled for the studio of Thomas Couture from a young age, so she was familiar with the ways of artists. While she accepted that her official role was to sit, or recline, in silence, she was also bold enough to question what Monsieur was doing and why. Why those flat strokes, those serious colours, why such impasto, why was yesterday's work good and not today's, so that it must be done again? What did Monsieur think of the Spanish painters, the Italians, the Dutch? Was that a Japanese print on his wall? What were his favourite flowers, his preferred fruits, which shades of red did he find most delightful? All this, while she lay half-naked on the day bed, conversing freely with the air of one quite equal to her employer!

Monsieur was both amused and intrigued by her manner. After some months he had decided to commence upon a life-size nude. Observing anew the black ribbon that Victorine wore habitually around her neck, he called her his 'Venus of the Bootlace', both in jest and admiration, which made her laugh. Now, Victorine would truly be his Venus, a goddess of love.

Some years earlier he had painted a study of the Urbino Venus by Titian, and this he hunted out from an old portfolio, and studied as the basis for his composition. At first, he directed Victorine to lie with her left hand on her knee, the near leg drawn up, the fingers of her right hand toying with a twist of hair. But after one drawing, it was clear that this pose did not altogether please him. He tugged at his moustaches, scratched a brush through his beard, paced the room, stopping before the Titian copy. There, the Florentine courtesan lies languid on crumpled sheets with her head turned in coy invitation, a bunch of flowers dangles casually from her right hand, while her left, at the meeting of her thighs, alludes to the source of her power. At her feet lies curled a sleeping spaniel and, beyond, two serving women occupy themselves with items of clothing in a pillared hall.

The studio was hot that day, and Victorine lay propped against two square pillows, silent but restless. From my usual position under the chair I could just see the soles of her feet, and noticed that her toes were twitching. I was intrigued by the movement, which resembled a wriggling nest of plump baby mice. Hunger and curiosity are the motives most associated with my kind, but it was purely in the spirit of adolescent playfulness that I lifted my head and crept forward on my belly a few careful inches.

Across the room, dissatisfied with his duplicate of Titian's coquettish nude, Monsieur sighed. 'No, no, no.' Victorine shifted upright, to see past the canvas on the easel. Her toes slid a little further from my view and I began to stalk them. Closer and closer I crept until I was just below the end of the chaise longue. I measured my distance, and – hop! – up I sprang!

Victorine gave such a shriek – she was entirely caught up with the matter of art and had forgotten our game. It seems my claws gripped more tightly than I had intended. Surprised at the disturbance, Monsieur lost for a moment his usual air of courtesy. 'Noiraud, you wicked creature! Get down from there immediately! *Vas! Vas t'en!*' He crossed the room and flapped his hand at me. Victorine raised her hand to protest that this was merely part of our game, but I mistook it for another rejection of my exuberance and, purely from instinct, my back arched with hostility and my fur rose into a million savage spikes.

Victorine laughed. Well, I jumped off the couch and ran for my dark corner under the chair. She tried to charm me from my retreat, but my dignity was wounded. Despite the temptations offered by fringed silk and soft words, I remained in seclusion for the rest of the afternoon, dozing until the studio was quiet and locked up for the night.

When I awoke it was dark, and I had quite forgotten the *contretemps*. I prowled the studio a while, caught and ate a fine mouse. The repast brought to mind Victorine's wriggling toes, and I placed myself eagerly before the canvas to inspect the progress of the scene. There she lay, the Venus of the Bootlace, her white skin glowing against the dark ground. Under the moonlight little detail was visible, and the head was merely blocked in, but already the image was characteristically Mademoiselle at her most assured. Her right elbow pushed against the crisp silk of the pillows, while its fingers caught at a Chinese embroidered shawl. Her left arm came across her belly to rest on her right thigh, emphasising lustrous curves, more honest than elegant. Her toes were blurs of white, idle against the creamy fabric, waiting for definition. But even unfinished, she was spirited enough to illuminate that tenebrous place.

In the tradition established by that purveyor of erotic

fantasy, Monsieur Ingres, a fair-skinned odalisque must be chaperoned by an African slave. A goddess of love, therefore, even a goddess of make-believe, requires her attendants; and so, in the following weeks, Victorine was presented daily with a bouquet of flowers by Fadéla, her Moorish friend, who complained that the pollen made her eyes water, and that laundry was easier work by far. Victorine's hair was dressed with an orange lily, her ears with pearls, and a heavy gold bracelet adorned her wrist. And her restless toes?

Monsieur regarded me, under my chair, from his position in front of the canvas. 'Fadéla,' he said, 'please fetch the blue and white slippers from the shelf above the bonnets.' He winked at Victorine, who smiled back. 'We cannot have our ambulating shadow distracted by all these little digits.'

Whilst Fadéla searched through the props, I jumped up onto the chaise for an inspection. Victorine leaned forward to stroke me and I arched my back under her hand, and waved my tail to show that all was forgiven. Monsieur narrowed his eyes at me. His exclamation this time was one of pleasure and discovery.

'Are you a spirit sent by Señor Goya to inspire me? I shall not ask you to hold your pose, little spy, but undoubtedly, a quantity of black paint and two gleaming yellow eyes will suit that bottom corner far better than some sleepy lap-dog. So be it.' He clapped his hands. 'To work! Fadéla, if you please!' And to this once more harmonious trinity Fadéla returned with the elegant slippers, and placed one dangling over the delectable toes of Mademoiselle Victorine's left foot.

Leg Money

She walked towards him down the street and a muscle in his chest went into spasm, perhaps his heart, maybe it was just indigestion, no, it wasn't. She walked bent over at a slight angle, a list to starboard, five or ten degrees, whatever, geometry wasn't his forte, but she inclined, gently at first, then more and more, and his heart went out to her, he felt it leave his chest and spread like margarine in a smooth slick through the air above the pavement until it reached her, wrapping itself about her, a pulsating butter-substitute halo. He found himself standing still, staring, as she came closer.

She put down the heavier of the two carrier bags with an epithet of sufficient strength to startle cats. Luckily there were none in the vicinity, unless in whimsical mood you counted as tabbies the two elderly ladies locking up the Save the Children shop, who were either too deaf or too well bred to make a thing about it, none of that ooh language young woman attitude. They fussed ostentatiously with the Yale and left at a brisk trot to get their bus, the subtitle 'full value for our OAP status' drifting opaquely in their wake. Watching them, she rubbed her hands, examining the effect of the over-stretched plastic handles which had creased her palms into relief maps of the Pennines. Why, she asked herself, and not for the first time, why am I carrying three two-litre tins of paint when with only a little further agony I could have cycled here with them strapped to my ankles, or conversely, what an amazing idea, phoned some friends who would have been only too happy to give me a lift, paint the hall with me, admire my crumbling plasterwork, and take me out to dinner afterwards. Silly me. She put down the other bag, straightened up and stretched out her arms in big circular gestures, butterfly stroke on dry land.

He blushed to realise that his initial thought had been snap!, that having missed the now obvious burden she was carrying his heart had leapt because he had seen her as, what?, deformed, mangled, flawed, as he was, and imagined that put her in his league, or he in hers, and his thoughts had already taken them to their first kiss, had slid them between cool cotton sheets in a country hotel, had seen sunlight touch her hair at dawn after a night of beauty and love. He blushed, though it didn't show, and hung his head, and then caught himself at it, thinking of himself as a blank space in the universe, as a faceless face in the crowd, a nobody, all because of his leg, his bloody leg, which made him limp and wasn't a problem to anyone but himself. He caught himself.

He looks nice, dark and brooding and sensitive, I wonder if there's something in that thing about being attracted to people who have lived similar lives, experienced similar pain. I wonder if he is in turmoil and scared and lonely and, oh really? What pain and turmoil do you think he's shared then? Don't be stupid, he's a man in the street, looking at the pavement, probably lost his bus ticket, probably drinks Fosters tinnies with the lads and belches advertising jingles for applause. Stop being the eternal bloody shepherdess looking for little lost lambs, look for a big kindly farmer who'll take care of you instead. Oh, he's looking at me.

He caught himself, and looked at her, properly, pulled his shoulders back and tried to stop his mind from whirring about. Focus. One thought at a time, come on. Yes, I'm looking and why not, she's got very grey and wonderful eyes, and she's looking back, I hope it's not the sight of me that's making her frown and curl her lip. I wonder if I watched her long enough would she stamp her foot and twist a piece of hair round her fingers and pout, but no, she's not Bardot, not a common or garden screen goddess, she's better than that, soft, touchable, sweaty, human.

Why is he still standing there? Perhaps he's lost, a tourist, a foreigner to these shores in search of our famed hospitality, and all he has of our language is the word for cheese or beer or single room with bath. High cheekbones, good nose, lovely hands, four o'clock shadow, or perhaps he's just starting a beard, or he's a George Michael fan, damn – oh shut *up*. Am I smiling?

I wish I'd shaved, she probably thinks I'm a tramp, no, tramps are outmoded, it would have to be one of the subset, Homeless, Poor, New Age, Transient, or something, but not with these boots, £80 boots, alright £39.99 in the sales, but still trendoid bootees. Fuck my footwear, any woman I'm attracted to in a deep and meaningful way won't be shallow enough to examine my feet for brownie points, she'll look at my eyes and my teeth, and whether

I button or zip, and how I laugh. I hope. I hope she has a sense of humour.

Have hours passed? If our eyes meet again will one of us speak? She hunkered down by her paint pots, enfolding the handles, preparing to start off. Why do I feel as though I'm six and he's holding the key to the universe, or maybe just a bag of sherbet lemons – I'm attracted to him, a total stranger, could be married, three kids, shacked up with an Annette Bening clone, and why would he look at me? He must have noticed my sturdy build, anyone with an eye can tell I'm wearing this scabby coat to hide the size of my arse, and I needed a haircut last year, so it's no use fluttering my eyelashes like Clara Bow. He's really quite handsome. Nice boots.

Deus ex machina, where are you now? Thanks a bunch for the Mini Metro in the side of the leg in Shepherd's Bush, spring '98, but could you just try to even things up a bit, give me a shove in another direction, beam me an opening line she hasn't heard before and won't turn up her nose at. Come on, toy with me, push me into conversation with as much random force as you pushed me onto the tarmac, give me another break, ha ha. If I had my leg money I'd be driving a car myself by now, bastard insurance. If I was driving a car I wouldn't be standing here looking at this woman and feeling like mush. I wouldn't be standing here feeling helpless and feeble and unable to take potential rejection because of a slightly squint leg.

Maybe I could stumble theatrically, do a sort of tomboy equivalent of dropping the lace-trimmed hankie, a quick jostle, an apology, and we'd end up talking, but I haven't got the nerve, it always looked so natural and easy in *Jackie* magazine when I was 14, but then so did eyelash curlers and frosted lipstick, and what kind of person throws themselves literally at a man these days? But maybe it's hormonal, and my body should not be denied its right to dictate events, even if my higher self finds it embarrassing and ridiculous. How would he look if I said, excuse me, but my Fallopian tubes are calling to you, my ovaries are yodelling?

Is she going to pick up those bloody bags? Am I going to let her, or am I going to be manly and step in and piss her off by offering help, though it might be she'd like some help, maybe she's moving house, leaving her past life behind her and starting afresh, and feeling strong and independent and whole, and if I say anything it would diminish that, and she might bite me. You cowardly sod. Do something, say something.

He's still standing there. Maybe he's waiting for someone in the video hire place, or he's going to mug the next little old lady who leaves the post office with a bulging handbag. Maybe I need therapy. Oh well. Time to go, time to abandon my dreaming and paint a skirting board.

His left leg, the bad one, trembled as he shifted his hip and took a step towards her. The other foot followed and suddenly he was in motion, slowly, approaching, looking down at her bent head where she genuflected on the pavement, weaving the plastic handles round her fingers in a Celtic knot. Pieta with poly bags, he thought, and his smile came up to his lips and into his eyes as he said . . .

'Can I give you a hand?'

S.W.A.L.K.

(SEALED WITH A LOVING KISS)

He didn't recognise the handwriting. Black ink, curvaceous, slender but bold, taking up almost the whole side of the padded envelope. A woman's hand? No return address. The orange sticker indicating recorded delivery heightened his interest. Ally had signed for it, on her way out at 7 a.m., and left it on the hall table.

He took the package into the kitchen, where the kettle had just boiled, and made himself instant coffee. The post was usually so predictable, mostly brown envelopes or bank statements, that he wanted to delay the pleasure of its opening a little while. He'd look in on Chloe first.

She waved her feet and fists at him, and warbled like one of those stuffed toys with an unlikely animal noise inside it. She seemed quite happy to lie for hours just looking at everything or, better still, sleeping. He was relieved, first babies were supposed to be little terrors. Not Chloe. Chloe was a little beauty, a little sweetheart, Daddy's little Munchkin, he told her, tweaking her toes, rubbing her tummy. She gurgled and smiled up at him. Funny now to think he'd never wanted children, adamant about it, too, through the course of several previous relationships.

Though Ally, when he'd met her, hadn't been keen either, quite happy without them, wanted to pursue her career. Despite her independence, she'd moved in with him after the first weekend. It didn't seem to him like being in love had always felt before, just – snap! – a feeling of being home. No great drama, more a steady surge that made him feel intensely happy.

When the hospital letter had come, Ally read it quietly, then showed it to him with tears in her eyes.

'If I have to have surgery, or laser treatment for whatever it is – God!'

'Hey . . . ssh, calm down, it's going to be okay, I promise. It's going to be fine.'

He hadn't known what he was saying, or whether she'd heard the words, but she leant in to him, and he cuddled her, cradled her head against his shoulder, stroking her hair the way she'd coached him. He picked up the letter, a card, really. Asking her to contact the clinic and her GP for further information. She sat up and blew her nose.

'Sorry. Silly to get so upset.'

'Well. They don't really say anything on this card, maybe it's just a precaution?'

She'd given him the look that said *what do you know, you're a man*, but she was still close to him, not angry at his attempt to be reasoning. He had to think rather carefully before opening his mouth with Ally, she was quick to spot latent chauvinism where there was only clumsiness on his part. He rubbed her neck.

'We'll take it one step at a time. I'm here with you.'

So few words with which to convey his love, so few that haven't been worn thin by previous owners. A sense of déjà-vu made him wonder if he hadn't watched this scene on television, an afternoon soap from Down Under, or an American cop show. Something with characters who spoke in statements. He'd tried it, and found that if you say a thing firmly, confidently, people will believe you and trust you – but just then that reminded him of Joanna, so persuasive herself, so angry at his seeming certainties. He didn't want to think about her, not now, here with Ally.

He had dried Ally's tears, and they'd talked about themselves, their future. Ally had said that maybe, after all, if she might lose the ability soon enough, she did want to have a baby, and he'd found himself agreeing, without a qualm. Whatever would make her happy, keep her feeling complete, must be good for them both. And once voiced, the idea became a focus so that, despite the gratifyingly low level of abnormal cells on Ally's cervix, the lack of risk, the time factor, their plan still seemed urgent. Chloe was conceived as soon as the treatment was completed.

And here she was, his daughter. Daughter, like wife, was a word that took some getting used to, but he loved it. He put a finger to her lips and she sucked. The force of it never failed to impress him. Not having much experience of other babies, he attributed her strength, her powerful desires, to inherited characteristics: his notorious efforts on the rugby pitch; arm-wrestling his father to defeat from the time he was a teenager; the womanising of his rakish youth.

He picked her up, took her into the kitchen and laid her in her crib on the armchair while he prepared milk. She talked to him in happy squeals and grunts, watching him move between the cooker and the fridge, then lost interest and reached up for the bright plastic mobile of ducks and chickens suspended from the mantelpiece for her amusement.

'Daddy's got a surprise, Chloe. Yes, look. What do we think it is, eh? Mmm? Shall we open it?'

Inside the bag there was a 60-minute audio cassette. He shook the bag, expecting a note, a compliments slip, perhaps, but there was nothing else. The tape was bare of any description.

'Somebody's playing a joke on us, aren't they Chloe?'

He put the cassette into the tape deck above the sink and pressed *play*, then settled Chloe on his lap to feed her. Her soft whooping noises, as she sucked milk and air, filled the silence, a counterpoint to the slight static hiss of the machinery.

'How do I begin? Ah, there's a song about that, isn't there? Isn't it the theme from *Love Story*? Probably the only seminal movie we never watched together, Mike. Appallingly corny, but apt. Anyway, this is me, Joanna, in case you've erased the past from your memory. At this point I know you're . . .'

He reached over and depressed the *pause* button. That cool, clear voice was a major part of why he'd fallen for Joanna. Soon after they'd met she'd gone to Greece for two weeks, and he'd called her answering machine at least once a day, just to hear her speak. Their mutual intoxication had been fed by the separation, they'd re-invented each other *in absentia*, and the eventual disenchantment was all the more bitter because the dream had been so powerfully constructed.

'I know you're thinking what the fuck does she want? And how did I get your address, and so on. Actually, I've always kept track of you, people have insisted on telling me your every move since we broke up. Besides, *why* is the thing you're worried about, isn't it?'

His temptation to eject the tape and throw it in the bin

was beaten by curiosity, just as she'd planned it no doubt. After the way they'd parted, he'd been sure he had nothing left to say to her and certain she'd never seek him out. Even as he acknowledged his interest, he recognised some of the old emotions stirring, almost found himself smiling at a sudden memory of Jo, naked and giggling, hurling shoes at him across the bedroom when he wouldn't get dressed.

'Well, stay tuned. How long has it been? Fourteen months, I suppose. A lot of time for anger to fade away. A lot of time to think. To talk. I went to see someone just to talk. I did really hate you for a while. But I'm not making this tape to chastise you, I wanted to focus on the good parts, so – well, I know it's a cliché and you'll think I do nothing but watch Oprah and read self-help books – I want to end the relationship properly. The closure thing. Mike . . .'

'Christ!'

Chloe, dozing, woke with a start at his expletive and tried to scream round the teat. He picked her up to burp her, walked her round the flat.

'Don't worry, darling, it's all over, she can't hurt us. Just a silly woman I knew, who can't let go.'

In soothing her he soothed himself somewhat. He put Chloe into her cot, watching with a twinge of envy as she settled into innocent sleep. Her nursery, once the dining room, was papered with pastel stripes, each colour boasting a different baby animal motif, and on one wall a huge pastel rainbow arced above the window, where ruched blinds resembled puffy clouds. When Ally had redecorated he'd thought it rather pleasing but looking at it now, through Joanna's eyes, he found the colours sickly and the whole thing too fussy.

He felt a little bit of confidence float away from him, as

though he'd been caught out, playing Happy Families. He'd always admired Jo's taste. From underwear, plain white silk or cotton, to wine, again white but expensive, she'd adhered to a discipline of buying the best, the classic, never the gimmick. That had flattered him, until he'd found his favourite shirts always 'in the wash', with only her choice available and ready to wear. She'd never let him slob around in her flat, tidying up after him in a way that used to amuse him, but finally became a cause of resentment on her part, tight-lipped obstinacy on his. Now he remembered that shoe-throwing incident differently. He had lain in bed in her flat listening to the phone ring while she was in the bath, so that she'd had to get out, dripping down the hall, to give the cold-call double-glazing salesman the benefit of her extensive vocabulary. Then she'd stormed into the bedroom to find him reading and given him hell, and his flying shoes for a finale. He hadn't liked that, hadn't liked it at all. What the fuck did she mean by contacting him like this?

'. . . Mike, please, don't get angry, just listen, please? I know you scorn all this stuff. You're so bloody balanced and you never had any patience with anyone less wonderfully capable than you – that's hard to live with. Is Alison perfect? Perhaps she is, lucky you. You'll probably have a perfect life, because you want that enough. And you deserve it. Absolutely. I always admired how determined you were, until it made me feel weak.'

There was a pause. He leant over to see if the tape was still turning, checked the volume, and was rewarded with a suddenly louder Joanna.

'Sorry, I said I wouldn't chastise you. I'm going to concentrate on the positive stuff now, okay?'

He moved Chloe's basket off the armchair, sat down, crossed his legs, folded his arms, jiggled his foot.

'Remember this?'

A piece of music, the theme from some film he couldn't recall the name of. Get to the point, Joanna.

'It's our song, Mike. *The Year of Living Dangerously* – even the title suited us. You took me to see it one wet winter afternoon, and it rained in the film too. Remember the bit where Sigourney Weaver goes to Mel Gibson's office soaked through and they take one look at each other and head straight for bed? Afterwards we tried to find Thai food but had to settle for Chinese, so we got a takeaway and went home to my place and ate it in bed, like Woody Allen and that girl with the thick eyebrows in *Manhattan*.'

Her memory for trivial detail amazed him. She probably knew down to the last bean sprout what they'd eaten that night, what socks he'd been wearing, whether they'd made love, and in what position. She'd even kept score of orgasms – 'that's six you owe me' – for a while, till it became a serious issue, and they couldn't talk about it at all, only yell, and cry, and slam doors. What doors the central heating hadn't cracked, she'd slammed to match.

'Remember the villa in Portugal? We drank *vinho verde* at that café where they only cooked sardines, and got pissed, and spent hours in the swimming pool with all the lights round it, but never had a hangover – and you said the only Portuguese you knew was 'haow naow braown caow' . . .'

A snort of laughter on the tape brought an echo from him. Her laughter was infectious and they'd often been rendered helpless by some obscure private joke.

'. . . and that time my aunt phoned, and I knew it would be her, but you grabbed the phone, you answered in a big deep voice, a Cockney accent, and said 'Sorry, missus, wrong number', and we were falling about screeching when she rang again and I tried to stop you but you got to it first and did a terrible Irish accent and she hung up, and it went on and on ringing but we were hysterical . . .'

He did remember. Jo biting a cushion, going red in the face, while he showed off. They'd laughed a lot. She could be pretty funny herself.

But how typically Joanna; she clearly hadn't stopped thinking about him since he'd moved out, while he hadn't thought about their time together from the day he met Ally. Hearing her voice again – well, it was painful, but he was glad she'd decided to put things right. It was an apology, really. She had always been slow to admit her faults. Now she'd learned some things about herself, maybe they could, well, not exactly be friends, but, perhaps he'd call her. No, he'd ask a mutual friend how she was doing, that would let her know he'd got the message.

'. . . you know, I'm glad I'm doing this. I was nervous about it. But if you've listened this long it proves I'm right about you. The You that's behind the Mike everyone knows. You've always liked to project an image of yourself as tough, to appear invulnerable. You told me once about your childhood – only once, God, I moaned on about mine constantly, but you were so, I don't know, secretive, reticent. Really compartmentalised. And that's what women mistrust in men, I think, their ability to prevent emotion from affecting their reason. You think it's a strength, to say to yourself . . . No, I'm not going to let this touch me. I don't want to change my view, or to change myself. Generalisation, okay, but it's pretty true.

'Anyway, maybe you were drunk, for once I don't

remember the exact details, but you were upset. You cried, in fact, you laid your head on my shoulder and you cried your heart out. There was a lot of stuff about your father, how you'd really idolised him till you were around thirteen. Then, you said, you saw him differently – you were as tall as him already, you were strong, you were stronger than him. He had a job he hated, and smoked forty a day to compensate. You saw him as weak. You said, and I quote – 'He's a failure, he never did what he wanted with his life and I'm not going to be a failure like him' – unquote.

'Why was he a failure? What made him weak, Mike? Did he love his family? Did he compromise his own ambition for a family he loved? Tell me, am I getting warm? You saw how he looked at you and you saw weakness. I wonder if he admired your arrogance, while you despised him? That must have hurt a lot.

'See, that's it, Mike, you are selfish and cruel and a bully because you want to be untouchable. But you're not, not now. Now you have something that makes you vulnerable, just like your father. Do you feel weak? Are you scared? Will your daughter grow up to despise you? Why did you get married? When did you change your mind about having kids? Was it just time? Was it hitting thirty-five? Spent all your life in training to be a cold bastard but having a family, that opened up your heart just a little bit, and now I can see all the way inside, and it's soft in there, Mike. You're just a big, soft sponge who's never been squeezed hard enough. All that gooey love stuff just trickling out of you, now you're a daddy. Stop me if I'm wrong, Mike . . .'

Something crawled down his cheek and dripped off his chin. He didn't move to brush away the tears, her smooth, clear voice held him fixed in the chair. Was it the mongoose or the snake that did the charming? There'd been a David Attenborough programme just the other day, but he couldn't remember now.

'. . . stop me if I'm wrong, but doesn't that make you just like your Dad?'

There was a little silence on the tape as it reached the end of side one, then a click as it automatically began to play side two.

A sigh.

'You know, recently I've become more like you. I keep my feelings in boxes now, as much as I can, lock out the stuff that might get to me. Things have happened in my life too, Mike. I'm not invulnerable either.'

The sound of rustling, the jerk and tear of tissues, he recognised at once. Ally did it too, reached for the Kleenex so she could go on arguing through the swollen eyes and blocked nose. When she'd finished, the floor around her would be strewn with twists of damp paper like a field of cotton.

'Listen, Mike. Listen. I don't have the heart to go on with this. My motives are too mixed. But there is something you have to hear. I've met someone. Actually we've known each other for a while, but very casually. He's become a good friend. We go for walks. He's just finished with someone too, you see. So we waited, wanted to be sure. And I suggested it, I said we should get tested.'

She was struggling to speak. He could picture her face clearly, eyes cast down, black hair falling over her face. He thought she must be sitting in her kitchen, at the table, resting her head in her hands now, her voice muffled, thick.

'Of course, I thought I was just being clever, careful. Being caring. There was nothing wrong with me. If anything he'd be – he'd be the one. But it didn't turn out that way. It was me. I was positive.'

In the hallway the phone rang, the answering machine picked up. Over the faint murmur of Ally's voice, Joanna's ragged breathing. She coughed, cleared her throat, blew her nose. Chair leg scraped against table as she got up and crossed the room to the sink, drank some water. Scraped as she sat down again. Tissues, again, noises in her throat.

'Used the wrong tense there, Mike. Am positive. Will be forever positive. I didn't sleep with anybody, I mean you were the last person. They say . . . the thing is, you have to get tested. I don't know a lot about this, how it works. It only happened . . . I only heard a few days ago. Anyway. It's up to you.'

She laughed, though he knew she was still crying.

'Nothing turns out the way you think, does it?'

The silence was different now. She was no longer there.

He sat still for a long time, looking at the tape spooling round until it stopped. He didn't know what to do. When Chloe woke up and began grizzling, he stirred. He hauled himself out of the chair like an old man, and went into the nursery. She was red-faced and her nappy was wet. He laid her on the mat while he undid her sleep-suit, removed the soiled nappy, cleaned her and replaced it.

Please stop crying, Chloe. He knew what she wanted from him. To be picked up and cuddled, to hear him speak in his special voice, but he couldn't do it. He couldn't speak. She looked ugly to him. Little red frog. Stop, Chloe. He found the pacifier and pushed it in. The phone rang again. Ally.

Chloe. She frowned up at him in silence, one hand raised, like a kid in class asking, 'Please? May I be excused?' Daddy's little Munchkin.

A Private View

It is a day for carefully chosen underwear, capaciousness and function rather than glamour, and with as little elastic left in it as possible. Marks & Spencer insist on believing that women should be waisted, but in Maureen's condition baggy is better, loose is more. Now, she's down to it, shivering, clothes on the chair, donning the paper robe. It resembles a coffee-filter in texture, completely A-line, like a bleached version of her old crimplene school dress. No floppy foam slippers to complete the ensemble, so she squishes bare feet back into her ankle boots, leaving the zips down.

The cubicle is designed on the principles of a starting gate. She is in limbo between the paddock and the hurdles. The door by which she entered leads back to the busy waiting area, to the coffee table piled with *Bella* and *Country Living* and pamphlets on beating cancer. The second opens into the world of Scientific Discovery, personified jointly by the subtle hum of humans and machinery.

She feels anxious, unsafe, needing to see what shape the room is, what makes the noises filtering under the door. She wants to assess the situation, be in control. What if she can't swallow what they give her, what if she throws up on the doctor's shoes? What if the room is full of students, their eyes at first impersonal, then zeroing in on her white legs, her poor muscle tone, every imperfection scrutinised? She's had those dreams about walking out naked onto a stage – walking semi-naked into a hospital theatre can't be much less terrifying.

Anxiety is normal. Well, some anxiety is normal. She ought to worry less. She worries about anxiety destroying her health and bingo!, a digestive complaint comes along to prove the point. Back into the self-blame cycle, stop it.

She gets up from the seat and looks in the mirror. Under harsh light her face resembles beef sausage with added artificial meat colouring under grey artificial skin. The whites of her eyes are yellow, or the white of her eyes is yellow? Maybe iridology is the next thing to try.

Footsteps approach, the cubicle door opens, and the light goes out, economically; the health service cuts are working. The nurse looks just like a nurse, not a man's idea of a woman in uniform, more ordinary, a woman to whom wearing suspenders to work would be laughable.

The nurse shows her where to sit and she takes a quick survey of the room. Four pale green walls around a huge piece of equipment and, in the corner behind her, a shielded booth for the X-ray technicians. The nurse departs and returns with a Nigerian doctor the size and colour of Yaphet Kotto. His English is formal, but his accent and his deep voice give unfamiliar emphasis to certain words, transforming his speech into a song that's hard to catch.

In innocent ritual she is offered white powder and asked to swallow it, as quickly as possible, not to open her mouth. It explodes as it meets her tongue, frothing violently on the lemon juice chaser, and she gags but gets it down. 'Good,' says Yaphet. 'Now please come. Please stand here. Place your feet here. Good.' She is pleased that he's so happy with her qualities of obedience.

And then she is on, beside, within, the contraption, her head turned to the left, left hand holding a beaker of gunk. It smells like a Bakewell tart, tastes like a warm, flavourless thick shake, the mother and father of all indigestion remedies. The good doctor gestures that she must drink it all.

'Keep swallowing, keep swallowing. Good. Turn onto your *left* side please, keep the legs straight.'

Motionless aerobics, effortless moving through space, as the bulk behind her leans and shifts. Her knees tremble a bit, the robe gapes at the back, but they say you can wear black to anything, so she stops considering her ancient underwear and looks at the nurse, approaching with a pillow, which is slid under a cheek as the machine tilts her horizontal. As though asleep and dreaming, a change of position sets Maureen's thoughts on a different tack.

It must be seven or eight years since she went dancing. Used to love it, kept her fit, kept her hip. She'd never expected to turn into the kind of person who, on catching *Top of the Pops* by accident would say, 'Who's that, and why are they making that terrible noise?' She let her mind flit across scenes from her youth – why were the seventies coming back? All those clumpy shoes, long hair with a centre parting, girls looking like the Mona Lisa without the smile. She'd never liked the era, the fashions, hated her life then, hadn't known how to change it. She'd always felt too old to be a real teenager, and now she feels really old, nearly middle-aged old, tired and sick and sick and tired of it.

'Turning onto your back now, legs completely straight. Good. Now onto your *right* side. Good.' She can't feel the process of the mixture within her, but Yaphet is watching. His eyes on the monitor, he rests his hand on her hip, ready to guide her through the next turn, twist, tilt.

When did she become old, then? When did it start, this new Maureen, so reclusive, so fearful? Poor health must have had some part in it, not feeling like dressing up, going out, not wanting to explain her reasons for staying in. She prided herself on enjoying her own company, but now she wonders, is she a hermit by choice, by nature, or by default? When she sees an acquaintance, as often as not she'll cross the street, duck into a shop. To escape – but escape what? As if life was meant to go on and on routinely, as if change was to be avoided at all costs. Self-protection. Lack of confidence. Perhaps it was all down to the nameless illness, her personal plague.

'Turning half onto your back. Not so far. Good. Now turning onto your *left* side, legs completely straight. Good.'

Last time she'd met someone new, someone possibly compatible, she realised afterwards that she'd prattled, related pointless anecdotes, laughed too much, tried too hard. The man probably thought her conceited. Out of practice, that's it. She envies those who have many genuine friendships, people they like to see often. Maureen knows herself to be, at heart, a one-man dog, a one-woman woman, putting all her eggs in one, possibly two, comfortable baskets. Great, if the basket is to hand. Baskets!? No, bad metaphor – her life experience is more akin to unworn Lycra, limits unknown. Life as a pair of pristine leggings, waiting to be stretched. Another great cliché coined.

'We are going to give you a little injection, to help the

muscles relax, okay? Good. Might affect your eyes a little. Okay. Good.' He inserts a needle into the back of her hand. There is no pain, but she feels tears threaten. To be cared for, to be treated gently but professionally, only illustrates the emptiness of her emotional landscape.

Last year's birthday present to herself was an aromatherapy massage, the surrender to confident touch a pleasure in itself, the relief from aches and pains lasting almost three days. Bliss, except that afterwards she kept crying whenever she heard music. Mahler was the worst culprit. She imagined that the experience had opened a sealed compartment of pain, stored up from the past like dusty junk in an attic.

As the machine tilts her again, she decides that no, life is not a pair of Lycra leggings. Life, capital L, is a pinball game. Somewhere in the great noisy machine there is a goal, but she's bouncing off the walls, falling, hitting obstacles and recoiling, with no game plan, manipulated by unknown forces, her illness making her a player of limited capacity, an imperfect sphere, her chances of hitting the targets diminished. She smiles a bit at the symbolism, and the graphic reality, as the huge machine beneath her shifts again.

'Moving onto your *right* side please. Good. Okay. Now, keeping the legs completely straight . . .'

The pillow is removed, the table tips her slowly into a standing position, and for the first time she can see the monitor, and on it her internal organs, a nest of monochrome snakes. A plumber would want to do something about those ungainly connections and multiple U-bends. Sharp intake of breath, shaking of head. Sell them for scrap, missus, you won't miss half of them.

The barium inside her feels heavy, like a new organ

displacing something vital. She sees it as an invisible lava-flow, curling and sinuous as a snake on a ladder. She wants to sigh, she wants to move, to curl up, to yell and run around, anything but be there, being investigated. The impatient patient. Yaphet's hand tells her to remain still, and she resigns herself to more introspection. Once more she fixes her eyes on her guts, her innards, coiled and twisted like the contents of a child's sock drawer, in which the medics can find no problem, despite the pain.

Maybe she's looking at the illness all wrong. Control is an illusion, not worth striving for. Chaos theory, fractals, the butterfly's wing – it's all about imperfection, the whole game is random, there is no pre-ordained path. Trying to impose structure, to control past, present, future, to keep from contemplating too deeply those things that cause fear, is utterly pointless. She is in the hands of a profession whose practitioners try like hell to avoid saying 'We don't know', so why does she care what they tell her? Why does she assume they'll come up with any answers, when they have yet to agree on the problem?

She remembers an economics class, twenty years ago, being told about spirals – the peculiar logic of it, how the economy was never stable, always spiralling upwards or downwards. Snakes and ladders. Maybe she's been in a constant series of spirals all her life, and can break out of the downward one now only by strength of will, some impossible act of faith.

Finally, Yaphet ushers her off the machine, tells her she may go away and dress. She wants to ask him 'So, do you have complete faith in Western medicine?' but his expensive training probably answers that one.

Her clothes smell of her, and it's a comfort to be back

inside her own soft shell, physical imperfections hidden from view. She looks at her face again, combing her hair. She'd imagined the journey of the barium lighting up her body from within, her eyes glowing like lamps, something from a Bugs Bunny cartoon, but there's no change, her face is still grim.

She can let herself out, this time, into the corridor, into the bland, beige waiting area. She takes a seat equidistant between crumpled pensioners and consciously straightens her back, slows her breathing, trying to relax her stomach.

In a few days she'll be told 'Well, good news, there's nothing wrong with you' again. She'll be expected to be relieved, but it will add to the anger that's accumulated over the months, the anger and frustration and depression which hurts, now, physically, in a new way. It does not help to be told so often, so indirectly, with such authority, that if she had a happier, more positive life, she'd feel better. How does someone get to that position? Can the NHS prescribe it?

'Ms Connelly?' She opens her eyes as the nurse breezes up. 'That's fine then, you can go home now, and we'll send the results on to your GP in due course, okay?' She could go home now, carrying away her enormous barium boa constrictor like a temporary pregnancy.

There's no one else at the bus stop, but the tail end of a number 41 disappears round the corner. Maureen swears, mildly. Bus scheduling; further evidence of random phenomena in a woman's daily existence. She's a long way from home. She can wait for the next one, or start walking. A dilemma. If she starts walking, perhaps it'll encourage the downward spiral of opaque mud in her intestinal tract. But if she starts along the road to the next stop she might miss a bus. If she stays still, who's to say another bus will ever come along?

From what little she knows of physics, matter is best left unobserved while it assembles itself into patterns, bus-shaped or otherwise. Rubbing her stomach, she sighs. It's a major choice. A major choice.

Not Rodin's Kiss

Harry walks Kay home from the party and she asks him in for coffee, regretting the words the moment they're out of her mouth. To her mind, courtesy of television drama, coffee is code for sex. Kay's heart bumps violently inside the slender framework of her ribs, echoed by the pulse in her neck, a giddying tempo. She curses herself for emitting the offer when she is sure she meant to say goodnight, but the internal logic centre refused to comply, the invitation has been issued. This is her first date for over a year and already she is adrift.

Harry stands close enough to create a warm zone, causing goose bumps on her neck, as Kay fumbles with her keys on the doorstep. She senses the hunger of his gaze: Harry Jones, Werewolf from Glamorgan, demon of the rugby field, six foot and square-built, a steak-fed prop forward at the peak of fitness.

Kay leads the way into the living room, switching on the art deco wall lamps, acutely aware of how invitingly the sofa glows, red and gold, how much the tufted white wool rug resembles the fleece of a sacrificial lamb. She tosses her keys onto the sideboard, calling over her shoulder, 'Have a seat. I'll just put the kettle on.' Harry stands at the hearth, slipping off his tweed jacket.

In the kitchen, Kay asks herself why she cannot speak the thoughts in her head. She feels she's adopted some pre-defined role, that a ritual is unfolding wherein the dance moves resist freestyle interpretation. Her choices were obvious, but the ability to make them has congealed, now that he's in her house. Soundlessly, she shapes the words 'I think . . . I'd like . . . could you . . . please leave now . . .' while the imp on her shoulder cajoles, 'Stop thinking . . . play it by ear . . . relax . . . isn't this what you want, you fool?'

She has the cold tap running full and fresh for filling the kettle when she senses body heat again. Convention dictates that she turn around and melt into his arms, but Kay is unable to move. Ambivalence glues her feet to the lino. Her body is stiff, her mind is syrup. For a second, a Kay dressed in red velvet, cut low and *Gone with the Wind*, succumbs to Rhett Butler, and an orchestra plays.

But the edges of the sink unit are hard against her knees, pelvis, stomach, and when she looks down at the torrent in the basin she's going over Niagara Falls in a barrel. So when Harry turns her round, hands twisting her shoulders until her hips must follow, she finds it difficult to respond to the imminent kiss. He is a stranger smelling of cologne and cigarettes and shampoo. His blond head looming towards her eclipses the kitchen light, throwing her into shadow. Failure to respond would be impolite, and though really quite good excuses – toothache, headache, heartache – spring to Kay's mind they are stopped by his mouth pushing at hers. If she permits her lips to part, to voice her reluctance, to ask for reprieve, she knows it could be taken as an invitation to penetration. So she kisses him very gently back, and his mouth is soft and rather nice at first but behind the plump tissue the teeth are hard, the jaws opening like the opposing halves of a monkey wrench. His tongue invades her, an alien in her mouth, a warm, wet creature with a mission, scouting for the platoon. As Harry probes her molars she feels panic stab at her guts, the reflexive cramping of internal organs, ugly sibling to the flutters of desire.

The ticker tape running through Kay's mind chatters 'please disengage', but, her mouth being possessed, she cannot express these sentiments to the possessor except by placing her fists against his massive chest and pushing. Harry loosens his grip on her mucous membranes and extracts himself with an audible squelch to show her a face of mixed euphoria and lust. In the shard of light reflected off the window, his eyes gleam like wet topaz, and his incisors shine very white in his grin. Despite herself, Kay is momentarily flattered that her passivity has been so stimulating, then, too late, alarmed, as Harry mistakes her own embarrassed 25% smile for encouragement and applies himself more vigorously to suffocation.

Harry is unfortunate in having done little research into the arcana of female sexuality other than that described in laddish magazine articles. Such fictions describe women as trembling with passion, saying no when they mean yes, loving to be treated manfully, and Harry, with only one thought in his whole being, is immune to the little telltales in Kay's behaviour which begin to signal her fear. He presses against her, one hand on the back of her neck, one hand kneading her breasts.

Kay has learned to avert her mind's eye from images of herself in the past as helpless, vulnerable. Through years of therapy, and the calm of celibacy, bold details have faded, the colour bleached out of painful moments, the power of teenage terrors paled. Now, that work is all undone. Instead of being prepared for the reality of attraction, she's spun back to become little Fay Wray wriggling in the grip of King Kong, virginal Chloe necking with muscular Daphnis in an urban setting.

'I'm only being polite!' screams Kay to herself, but meanwhile her tongue has had to move to make way for Harry's determined embouchure. She discovers her hands are gripping the draining board behind her, that the rush of noise is the running tap, echoing the blood which whirls round the inside of her skull. She opens her eyes, amazed to realise she had closed them in unwitting parody of every kiss she'd ever seen on film, every piece of sculpture designed to convey rapture in cool, marbled elegance.

From the corner of her left eye, beyond the butterfly flicker of her lashes beating on his skin, Harry's pores glisten. Breath rasps violently through his nostrils, hot against her cheek. Harry slides a hand under her shirt, takes her bottom lip between his teeth, and there she is, pinned for consumption, like a tiger's breakfast. With a tiny whimper, Kay's muscles slacken fractionally, and as she yields that first boundary, her eyelids flicker and, finally, close. Tight.

Her Drug of Choice

A CAUTIONARY TALE FOR TRAVELLERS

The bookshop is Laurie's last stop before passport control and the security gate. She swerves into the carpeted lay-by so that the couple behind her, who've bickered since check-in and all the way up the escalator over the cost of IKEA versus Habitat curtains, might pass ahead. Laurie registers an inner smirk at being civilised enough to avoid such disharmony, and not just because she is travelling alone. Had Mark been flying with her, instead of surveying bridge footings somewhere on the Humber estuary, she feels sure their eyes would have rolled in unison.

Laurie's scornful mood intensifies as she browses. She loves bookshops, but not in airports, resenting any implication that reading matter is a mere travel accessory. She pauses at a display intended to seduce female readers. The covers are garnished with fragile sling-backs and dinky little handbags and toy poodles, martini glasses and lipstick kisses, tangled bikini strings and powder-compacts featuring kittens or the Eiffel Tower. With the exception of the poodles, Laurie actually likes most of these items as originals, has even collected a dozen 1950s' compacts, and she deplores the retro-pastelisation – very pleased with this sudden coinage – of summers past.

Stepping away from the gender-biased arrangement, her eyes light on an array of better fare; Margaret Atwood, William Boyd, Jonathan Carroll and on through the alphabet until S where she spots Muriel Spark's *Loitering with Intent*, and smiles at the irony. She'll loiter no more; her flight is being called and as her intent is to spend the next week with her beloved Mark in a three-star hotel in Hammamet, novels will be totally superfluous. In any case, Mark has increasingly warned her about this fiction addiction leading her away from real life, and to answer his point Laurie has brought just one slim volume for the outward journey, appropriately Neil Jordan's *Night in Tunisia*, an old favourite, which she has devoured before the plane touches down in Tunis itself.

Only two hours later, Laurie suffers acute cravings for the narcotic of literature. Mark's fax, awaiting her at the hotel's reception desk, apologises for having missed his own flight due to work complications and forecasts a delay of 24 hours, possibly 48, before he can join her. Laurie has affected insouciance. She has traipsed round the shimmering pool, located both restaurants, dithered in the gift shop – postcards, towels, sunscreen, brass trinkets, poorly translated guide books, but no fiction. She has admired the tiled Arab Tea Room, gazed at palm trees, unpacked her case, and managed to keep panic at bay with some light humming. But as fellow guests proceed to dinner, she is miserable and a little bit angry with Mark. Instead of couscous by candlelight and a moonlit stroll on the white sand of the private beach, she endures a solitary ham sandwich from room service by the fitful illumination of CNN news. Their room – *her* room, she corrects herself bitterly – is a white box filled with two double beds, a wall-mounted TV, and one spindly chair. It has a view of the gardens and, invisible beyond them in the dark night, the sea, whose continuous conversation with the shoreline provokes in Laurie a nagging melancholy. If only she had a book, a good book, she thinks she could avoid emotional meltdown.

At 10 p.m., the hotel's public spaces are still peppered with guests, some in the kind of garments more suited to a jungle trek than a beach resort, others already committed to their North African experience in garish souvenir *djellabas*. Waiters in white Zouave leggings traverse the foyer with trays of drinks and large items of luggage. Laurie saunters through the lobby scanning notice-boards until she finds the name of her tour operator tacked above a desk, where a tidy display of brochures advertises camel rides, trips to Carthage, and guided tours of authentic *souks*. Under the desk a shelf bears tourist flotsam; a broken plastic comb, a child's blue sandshoe and a few tattered paperbacks. Laurie's heart lifts and swiftly plummets as she sees the names on the spines. Robert Ludlum. Sven Hassel. Jilly Cooper. Faye Kellerman. She fingers the warped, grey corners of a Catherine Cookson with a grimace.

'Everything is okay?' A member of staff appears at her elbow, a middle-aged man with dark eyes and slim moustache. Laurie tries not to think immediately in terms of resemblance or otherwise to Omar Sharif, but fails – they could be cousins. She pictures him astride a speeding camel in *Lawrence of Arabia*, then in a tender scene from *Dr Zhivago*. While she processes this cinematic trivia, the man kindly assures her of every assistance if only she will name her desire.

Laurie hesitates to ask about finding a bookshop in some nearby town, knowing perfectly well that she doesn't have the courage to go anywhere without Mark. Excusing herself politely she drifts towards the lounge bar, where guests of a certain age cluster like sponges on a reef. Grey-haired and leather-skinned they sit, in groups of four or six, drinking gin and discussing cars and golf, the Canaries versus the Algarve, investments and pensions, to the tinkly plinky-plonk of homogenised Bacharach. Laurie wanders towards the Arab Tea Room downstairs, where a younger crowd perches on emerald green pouffes, sipping Coke and cracking pistachios, chattering against a din of ethnic rhythms. She can visualise herself here with Mark, but she won't go in now.

Exiting, she bumps into a body, puts up her hand and is disconcerted to find it cupping a warm – and quite decidedly surgically-enhanced – breast. It's the female of the arguing couple off her flight. 'Terribly sorry,' whispers Laurie, embarrassed. 'S'okay,' laughs the woman, and slithers by in a waft of perfume. Her companion is close behind, one finger tucked possessively through his partner's turquoise thong where it crests tight Capri pants. Plodding back to her lonely cell with a Ludlum tucked into a trouser pocket, Laurie ponders her growing capacity for envy, snobbishness and, in terms of literature, shameful compromise.

Next morning, the aromas of coffee and toast summon Laurie to the breakfast room buffet. She totes the Ludlum as armour against intrusion or pity and pretends to read, though last night's experiment has not converted her to his talents. She takes grapefruit segments and a croissant to the only free table and eats listlessly, her head buzzing with the babble of accents from Birmingham to Bremen.

With the detested novel and a bottle of water Laurie wanders out to the pool's edge, looking for a shady spot.

The chairs and loungers are all claimed by towels and beach bags, though at 9.30 a.m. only a handful of guests are using them, and no one is yet in the water. Feigning the benevolent gait of a Stepford Wife, Laurie putters round the gardens, hoping to find some generous, approachable soul with a book they might be willing to lend. Soon, she spots the arguing couple. They sprawl in the shade of a parasol, apparently asleep, she in a shiny white bikini, he in knee-length zebra-striped shorts, their hands entwined. On the ground beneath their loungers sits a basket, and within it a book. No, two books. Laurie's stomach flutters at such proximate treasure. The woman shifts her head a little, yawns, stretches her slender, silver-tipped toes, and relaxes. Laurie moves close enough to scan the titles, not expecting much, and is wrong. Paul Auster's *Oracle Nights* and Brian Moore's *The Magician's Wife*.

This evidence of failure in her habitual cataloguing of the human race causes Laurie a quick pang of humiliation, rapidly overcome by greed. She would like to read both these novels, considers waking their owners and forcibly befriending them, suggesting a trade. But trade what? She could only offer a plain bracelet, her best swimsuit, a brand new jar of Clinique moisturiser. For a moment she sees herself as an eighteenth-century adventurer buying important tribal curios with cheap glass beads but rejects the comparison. Nonetheless she can foresee this woman – a woman who seems to appreciate good writing – gawping at such a bizarre idea, disinterested, or more likely contemptuous, laughing at Laurie's pitiful booklust.

She walks on. Behind her shades, her eyes are alert for other readers. She wonders if she might appeal to some as fellow addicts, and rehearses angles of approach which will not represent her as an irrational nut. There is no chance to enact these scripts, though, as the guests who gradually emerge to flop onto reserved loungers seem keener to talk and snooze and anoint their flab with cocoa butter than to read. One of the elderly Germans has a tabloid newspaper, and a big blonde woman scribbles with fierce concentration in a pamphlet of Dutch crossword puzzles. Perhaps, thinks Laurie, I chose the wrong kind of holiday. Where, oh where, are the others of my tribe?

As the sun rises higher in the cloudless sky, Laurie slumps on the hot paving with her back to a wall, and analyses her plight. She is in a circle of hell specially reserved for fiction addicts who have turned up their noses at the habits of others. She fears that like Ray Milland in *Lost Weekend* she will deteriorate mentally if she doesn't soon get her fix. She might even hallucinate books, as those wandering in desert climes tend to hallucinate oases. Books about North Africa, books about sand and heat and stupid mistakes. Laurie swigs some water, wipes the sweat from her face with a sleeve. It is only half past ten. She swivels round and lies flat, with the chunky Ludlum as a pillow, closes her eyes, and allows the heat to beat down upon her just for a minute.

The sound that wakes her is a gong being struck, and a perky Australian voice summoning guests to an indoor exercise class guaranteed to whet appetites for lunch. Laurie sits up, startled, from a ghastly dream of going blind, to discover she *is* blind, can see nothing except white sparks. Her limbs are heavy, her body clammy and malodorous. Holding on to nearby bushes, she gropes her way towards a hazy patch of darkness, a blessed parasol, and under it a vacant lounger. Lying back with eyes shut, she fumbles to open her water bottle and takes a deep draught. She tries opening her eyes again. Through slits the world glows Martian red, then orange, then gold until in fine gradations the scene becomes clearer to her. Fearless pensioners with crocodile hides bask in the shallows of the pool and under the breakfast-room awning small figures sip drinks and munch fried snacks. Laurie would love a drink, an ice cream, anything cold and sweet, but the journey to the freezer is quite unthinkable. She flops back again, exhausted, letting her arms fall where they may. She's lying on fluffy towelling, and as her left hand droops off the recliner it rests upon an open raffia bag. Her fingers decipher the shape of plastic bottles, presumably sunscreen lotions, and then two hard, square-edged shapes. Books. A surge of glee shoots through her, banishing fatigue. She inches the coveted tomes onto her lap and, without looking down, yanks at the fabric beneath her until she has covered herself to the waist. Leaning forward, she sweeps the whole bundle into her arms, and proceeds very, very carefully towards the distant, sombre entrance to the accommodation block.

When she remembers it later, there was a brief moment of lucidity around midnight, when nausea sent her staggering to the bathroom. In the artificial light at the sink she watched a violently pink visage staring back at her, and did not believe it was her own. But what she mostly remembers is the feverish dream of being pursued by Omar Sharif across a red desert, the padding of his camel's feet loud in her ears, the endlessly retreating caravan of tuneful ice-cream vans and wavering palm trees, forever out of reach. Then, the moment when she woke again, hours later, to find Mark's pale, concerned face peering down at her, the sensation of his hand on her brow, and a terrible stabbing pain in her back and legs.

'You're so dehydrated, you poor honey. Here, try to sip a bit of water . . . I'll call down for a doctor . . . woah, not too much now.' And as she moves weeping into the haven of his arms, she is not too delirious to miss his expression turn – just for a moment – to disbelief when, in the tangle of sodden sheets, he spots her stolen bounty. A pictorial history of German tanks, and an Elizabethan saga by Jean Plaidy, in Dutch.

Statutes & Judgements

There are twenty-three possible D Christies in the phone book. I exclude the dozen who live too far outside the city centre to commute, and the ones who give their full names. The one I'm looking for doesn't volunteer information. Of course, some of those Ds might be discreet Dianes, Doreens, Dorothies. Pulling out a city map, I circle the areas corresponding to the telephone exchanges. Should I call every one of the twenty-three, or find some other way to narrow down the search?

I know his work number off by heart now, and call the switchboard.

'Can you tell me what time you stop work?'

'Which department were you wanting?'

'It doesn't matter, could you just tell me when everyone leaves the building?'

The woman sighs.

'You'll not get anybody at their desk after 4.30, dear, and it's nearly that now.'

I grab coat, scarf, keys and run down the four flights of stairs to the street. The building is only a couple of blocks away; if I'm quick I might spot him leaving. Which exit will he use? If I stand halfway down the street, in the doorway of the closed sandwich shop, I'll be unobserved and still have a fair chance of seeing any sign of mass exodus. Just as I reach the shop it starts to rain, and I'm glad of the excuse it gives me to cover my hair with the scarf.

The street is quiet. Next door, the proprietor of a second-hand TV shop stares out into the darkening sky. From my doorway I see children's programmes on five sets in his window, racing on two more. It looks sunny in England.

A trickle emerges from the mouth of the office complex and becomes a stream of moving people, umbrellas blooming instantly in the warm rain. I press further back into the doorway, as groups of men and women, hunching shoulders and tugging at their collars, straggle past. What will he be wearing? I saw only his face and upper body at the interview. Green shirt, straggly brown hair, a full mouth, strong nose, eyes partially hidden behind tinted lenses in a silver frame. I look for someone with glasses and a cigarette, remembering my fear as I'd watched his tobacco-stained fingers flick through my dossier only a few hours ago.

Department of Social Security is a misnomer. Let's call it something real, let's call it Department of Just Doing My Job. Waiting, in the sweat-scented, smoky anteroom, I'd run through a dozen alternatives, lyrics to the rhythm of my pounding heartbeat. I'd felt as though I were running a fast mile sitting still, anticipation drying my mouth and throat, head full of parts of sentences, a jumble of half-truths and excuses. Not knowing what I'd done wrong but suspecting that my own habitual guilt would condemn me if I let it show, was no frame of mind in which to be interrogated.

The sun emerges weakly, causing an incongruous rainbow to appear in the leaden sky, low over the huge concrete DSS monolith. My mouth twists at the irony. Pot of Gold. The State Will Provide. To Him That Hath Shall Be Given. While I think my thoughts the flood dries up, people grouped in puddles at bus stops evaporate. I've missed him. Just as well, perhaps. Wait. Two men come through the reception area, pausing to exchange a joke with the guard at the door. Both wear padded nylon jackets and have dark hair. The smaller might be D Christie. They leave together, walking uphill, and I follow at some distance. The taller man stops outside a pub, inclines his head. The possible D Christie shakes his head, waves goodbye, starts back down the street. When he passes, I catch the reflection in the window, super-imposed on a clutter of surfboards and neon-bright wetsuits, the glint of his spectacles, hand to mouth, inhaling smoke. The smell of hot cigarette lingers behind him like a fart. Now he's moving, checking the time, and I'm sure it's him, the set of his head, even the back of it, producing a sensa-tion in the pit of my stomach that is recognition. He crosses the road, glancing at the traffic, running a little to reach the pavement before the approaching taxi barrels past. Delayed by several more vehicles, I lose sight of him for a moment, and walk the length of the street twice, anxiously scanning, until I practically hug him as he emerges from a small deli-catessen. I dip my head and enter the shop he has just left, pause for a few beats and then leave, to see him stuff a pint of milk into one pocket of his jacket, a battered paper bag containing floury white rolls into the other.

He leans flat against the wall by the bus stop, and I have nowhere to hide. In panic I search my pockets for props and come upon sunglasses, a little pretentious but good enough as a disguise. Self-consciously aware of my sudden resemblance to Françoise Dorléac, I too lean, casually, against the wall, sneaking glances at my quarry from behind the dusty brown lenses. He smokes a Gauloise. D Christie as Yves Montand. D Christie as Eddie Constantine. Will he suddenly break into song? Get Marcel Carné in here to direct this and we could have music and a happy ending. My fantasy is arrested by the arrival of a bus.

He gives me no more than a quick once-over as he merges with the head of the queue. I smile to myself, acknowledging that this lack of recognition reflects his attitude to his work, to me. I push a bit to get close enough to eavesdrop on his fare, then take a seat two back and across the aisle. I reassess my victim.

Item: the label from his maroon jacket sticks up at the back.

Item: he has dandruff on his collar, hair that needs cutting.

Item: he has just surreptitiously picked his nose, inspected the result and wiped it on the seat.

Item: he is whistling through his teeth, and the tune is undoubtedly Robert Palmer's most recent macho anthem.

These things are sufficient, with what I know of him, to reinforce my instinct for retribution.

Where is he going? The bus enters a part of the city with which I am not familiar, passes shops selling shoddy goods, three for a pound, brand names too obscure to boast about. For a moment I'm on holiday, a tourist abroad without fixed agenda, free to take pleasure in the strangeness of my journey, the little frisson that comes of adventuring beyond known territory. The weak evening sun is almost hot through the glass. I turn into it, warming my face, gazing out without focus. There is a stillness now inside my head, replacing the tinnitus of fear. It would be the most pleasant thing in the world to go on forever riding round and round in this bus, in constant suspension of time. I could almost forget.

I think again of the letter, the bold signature under p.p. Area Manager, the confident officialese.

During the interview he'd told me he was just doing his job, it was nothing personal, and I'd believed it, believed there was no plea I could make that would alter the finality of his decision. The finality of his green shirt, his big mouth. The stubby spatulate fingers, yellow and brown in places from his disgusting habit. The form I'd refused to sign. Moral right versus legal right. He hadn't understood. That shake of the head, pursing of lips, was he Pontius Pilate in a former life? Just doing his job. What kind of security does that imply?

The seat behind D Christie becomes vacant and I move into it. I count the moles on the back of his neck, note the shape of his ears, the thinning hair at the crown of his head, inhale and exhale in his rhythm, wondering that he does not sense our closeness, that he shows no intuitive qualities. Part of the contract of employment. Give up your sixth sense at the door, sign here, you can have it back with your enhanced Civil Service pension and gold-plated carriage clock when we're eventually privatised or you're made redundant, whichever comes first. D Christie, on the dole. How would he manage on £44 a week? How would he manage if they took even that away from him? Suspension. Suspension of life.

He gets up. The bus swings wide round a corner, accelerates to a stop, causing passengers' knuckles to whiten as they grip seat-backs. I tag after him down a street of grimy stone tenements, testament to the city's log-jam of housing repairs. The pavement is strewn with refuse, fag ends, crisp packets, and a child's sugar-pink scooter lies abandoned in the gutter outside number 14, which D Christie enters. I walk past, return on the other side of the road, using the phone box as a hide. A light goes on in the top flat, behind short orange curtains. Projecting from the window is a For Sale sign, the agent's number too small and too distant to read.

It is gratifying to find a phone book still in reasonable condition. D Christie, 14 Eskbank Drive. I need to re-acquaint myself with his voice, to torment him a little.

'Hello, is this the flat for sale?' I have watched enough *Brookside* to be sure my accent is passable.

'Er, yes, yes, it is, actually, yeah.'

'Would it be possible to see the flat this evening, like?'

'Er, well what time would you be wanting . . .'

'Sorry, the thing is, I'm waiting on my husband getting back, he works late on a Thursday. Would about 10.15 be okay?'

'Tonight? You couldn't make it Sunday, could you?'

'Oh, I know my husband's very keen, he said it's right where we want to be, top flat and everything, I mean we'd be looking to make an offer tomorrow if we liked it, so . . .'

'Right, right, well okay then, some time after ten, and the name is?'

'Er, Lennon. Mr and Mrs Lennon. Thanks.'

He doesn't question the direct call instead of a viewing through his estate agents, must be desperate to sell. In the dying light, I look at the dirty street, the neglected patches of garden, and don't blame him for that.

In all my anger and frustration, my desire for revenge, I have thought no further than this point. I know where he lives – and now what? Until something has been resolved I will not entertain the safe, sensible alternatives – forgetting the whole thing, buying a bag of chips and spending the evening, and probably the rest of my life, in front of the TV. I will not plan to return another day. Spontaneity, long diminished by the restrictions my income has placed on my expectations, fuels me now to do something extraordinary. I desire to impede the course of D Christie's life as abruptly as he has altered mine. And the train of events, finding him, following him, confirming my judgments on him, are all falling into place so beautifully. Never put off until tomorrow what you can do today.

A gas leak? A flood? Report of a suicide attempt? These things are too transient, simply inconvenient to have to explain to the emergency services. How angry do I feel?

Scroll back three months. I'm standing in a dark street, not unlike this one, looking up at a window. Inside, a couple dance, kiss, laugh. I have known the man intimately during the past eighteen months. Since then I have stood here often in the dark, replaying in my head the final scene between us. My tears, his coldness. My pleas, his judgement. All he'd left behind was a sock under my bed. The letters returned unopened. At times, I'd lain in wait for him, followed him, suffered his fury, his verdict that I behaved like a victim, that I was insane, that I wouldn't accept the truth if it slapped me in the face. He had a strong face, a strong personality, so strong he sucked away my confidence and left me weak. Too weak to be angry. Then.

Outside the smelly phone box night is falling rapidly, and beneath the sodium lighting the street looks a perfect setting for crime. At the far end the light is stronger, for there are shops, a pub, a chippy and a Chinese takeaway. Here, by D Christie's house, the light is poor. I cross the street and enter the stair. At the back of the building a passage leads into a communal drying green. I climb to the brightly lit first landing. The upper floor lighting has been seen to by previous vandals, but the first floor light still functions, despite the dents and cracks. Removing my shoe, I whack at the plastic cover two, three, four times, hard enough to disturb the filament and put it out of order. In a cold sweat, I expect the hand on the shoulder, the shout through the letterbox, but compared to *Top of the Pops* it has made hardly a sound. The stair is quite dark now. I go up and pause for a while outside D Christie's door, putting my ear to the letter flap. Television, advertising jingles.

I return to the passage and sit on an empty crate. It's a gamble; if he doesn't leave the flat a frontal approach will have to be devised. But I have confidence in my assessment of his character. In fact, I feel almost happy. After the waiting game, the interview, action is more than a relief. Perhaps there's something in voluntary work after all.

I examine the contents of my pockets. Tissue, three bus tickets, keys, purse. The sunglasses, a brooch with a broken pin. I find two Polo mints and divide my rations, one now, one for later. I count how long it takes on one side of my mouth for the molar to react to the sugar, then switch to the opposite cheek and count again. Attempting to recall in detail every check-up since I lost my milk teeth occupies me for a while.

My backside is growing numb when I hear movement on the stair. Footsteps descending, a voice cursing the lack of visibility. The faint silhouette as the person steps onto the street has me on my feet and following. I know those ears, that walk. My quarry makes straight for his local. The cheap velvet curtains afford me glimpses of the interior, and I am pleased to see him greeted with a nod by the barman, hailed by couples at a corner table. He takes his pint across the room to join them. Above the bar, a clock reads 7.52 p.m. I feel safe in assuming he'll be there until close on ten. In two hours I can surely find what I need.

In fact it takes only minutes to find a skip, to reach in and arm myself. I hide my prize in a doorway while I backtrack to the corner shop to get a samosa, then take my supper and my other valuables back to D Christie's tenement. The hours pass, slowly, time black as pitch, black as coal. I can just about see my own hands, down here in the murk, gnawing my vittles. I am nervous, as I had been before the interview; dry mouth, sweating palms, racing pulse. Waiting again, the old enemy.

Soon it is quiet on the street. Not much of a moon. About now D Christie will be taking his leave of the Old Bellevue Bar, grinding his last Gauloise to ash, the premature sale celebration flooding him with good cheer. He'll come back needing a slash, and hoping to give the air time to clear in the toilet before his potential buyers ring the doorbell. Maybe a wee cup of coffee before they arrive, to cut the smell of beer and sober up a little. Not that he needs it, he can hold his drink with the best of them, D Christie. He whistles something or other the pub band played, on the tip of his tongue, come on, it's a standard. Nah, it's gone. Fuck, this stair's dark.

He starts up the first flight, unaware of his shadow. When he reaches the landing his shadow flattens to the wall until he grabs the banister and hauls himself up towards the next floor. Too many fags, D Christie. The shadow takes on a curious shape as it slides after him, its hands engaging in some sort of puppet-dance of manipulation. Halfway up the penultimate flight he gets dizzy, pauses for breath, leaning his head against the cool, scarred wood of the banister. Perfect.

The brick hits him at the nape of the neck, just where his hair starts to fuzz and grow down onto his shoulders. It makes a soft clunk, echoed by the whoosh of air as he gasps, trying to lift his head. His hands still grip the wood, he's leaning away from me, each foot twisting on its toes, arching his back against the railings, but he doesn't really want to see because he raises one hand to his eyes. Chicken. I grasp his knees and pull up, so that his hip slides onto the banister, then he's on his back, hands flailing. He doesn't offer much resistance, or maybe I'm too quick for him, too efficient. Will I, won't I? I tuck his feet under my elbows, his legs are stiff, straight beneath my breasts, it's just like playing wheelbarrows. Here goes. One good hard shove. His knuckles rattle the railings on the way down and a faint whisper, a question, issues from his lungs before he hits the concrete.

What did you want to say, D Christie? Why? Why me?

Silence. Nobody cracks open a door to shed light on the situation, nobody pursues a neighbourly impulse to see if all is as it should be at 14 Eskbank Drive. A religious addiction to *Taggart* holds them in thrall. Nothing like crime to keep you in your seat. I look down into the stairwell but can discern no movement. Picking up my brick, I start down.

He lies on his back, looking strangely soft and boneless, a flounder. I am not indifferent to his fate. I wouldn't say I was indifferent. A great one for following through, completing the task, tying up loose ends. So, despite the need for caution, I move closer. His eyes are closed but flickering. A tiny noise in his throat alerts me. I bend over him just enough to hear, if he should speak. One word. 'Lennon.'

The walk home is long, the night has turned chill. I concentrate on keeping the final Polo mint away from my molars. On the principles of 'The Purloined Letter' I chuck the brick into a skip in a housing action area, where it looks just like any other brick. If bricks could talk, I think, dusting off my hands, what would this one cry out?

D Christie didn't cry out. D Christie was not a man to volunteer information.

Time Goes By

'Next year,' shouts Colin, 'we're hiring a big house some-where, Fife, probably! Get everyone together there for New Year! It'll be fantastic!' His breath roars hot and peaty across my face.

'Great!' I yell, trying not to flinch. We have our backs to the sink, classic wallflowers. I sip at a tea-cup full of cider, wishing I were home in bed, but with this noise coming through the walls sleep would have been elusive. Colin's girlfriend Janice is visible through the doorway, dancing in the living room, her cleavage heav-ing between black spaghetti straps, a pink feather boa trailing underfoot.

Across the kitchen counter a couple talk. She is dark-haired and tall, with tears in her eyes. Her boyfriend tries to get her to smile. She shakes her head, looks at her feet. Bare toes in gold mules in December. He slings a muscular arm round her and they move to the hallway and out onto the landing. My guess is they are breaking up. Hey! Happy New Year, I don't love you any more.

'So, have you made any resolutions, then, Helen?' Colin has run out of real conversation and so have I.

'The usual – you know, learn Spanish, do yoga, change my entire life.'

'Aye, that's you sober and organised, but come on, what about your dreams? Tell me your dreams!'

A glance at Colin's beer gut and Hilfiger shirt suggests my dreams would bemuse him.

The music stops suddenly and Janice shrieks 'The bells, the bells!' like a demented Quasimodo, opening the bay windows. Colin shoulders his way to the TV and clicks to ITV, where men in whirling kilts and women in spangly dresses are reaching a frenzied climax accompanied by the Tam White band.

'5, 4, 3, 2, Happy New Year!'

On screen, two C-list co-presenters kiss politely. Outside, ships in Leith Docks sound their horns to welcome the Millennium and fireworks light the sky to an amber haze. Janice and Colin go lip to lip, while the singles whoop and exchange random smooches. As I slip out and across the landing to my flat, the unhappy girl from the kitchen runs down the tenement stair alone, gold mules clattering.

In my own kitchen, I make tea, and sit by the window. The noise from next door becomes an anonymous thumping bass that travels via the floorboards up the chair legs into my bones. After a while it's background, as I muse on previous Hogmanays. There was the time I went to the Tron Kirk, young enough to enjoy the mad squash of strange bodies; the year I slept through it all on cold medication; the one where Stella came round and we drank tequila and cried over Bogart and Bergman's *Casablanca* dilemmas. And last year, with James. The party at his painting studio where, as midnight arrived and I turned to look for him, I saw that he was not looking for me. Happy New Year, you don't love me any more. I could have said it then, if I'd been honest. So could he. We waited another three months for confirmation.

We'd planned a weekend in March to travel north. His choice of music deterred conversation until we reached Fort William and the CDs ran out. We turned off onto single-track roads and soft rain began to fall. It was cold, but I had the window open on my side, watching the rain gullies, white against the darkening hills, and bracken shivering in our slipstream. I found the silence and the smell of wet countryside exciting but when I looked at James his face registered a familiar 'Why am I here?' expression.

The tell-tales; all those things you see in a person whose habits you think you know well. Impatience, avoidance, tiredness, vanishing libido and sense of humour. The fact that their eyebrows seem different, their hands. Their mouths, where once you read generosity and beauty, now betray bitterness, selfishness, pomposity. Intuition is a language too difficult to translate, a dialect you rarely trust yourself to interpret.

The following morning we'd got up shivering and lit a fire, explored the cottage and watched drizzle through fogged windows. By midday it stopped and we went for a long walk down by the loch. The shoreline was narrow and pebbled, and we skimmed stones, then sat on huge yellow-lichened boulders to contemplate the landscape. James lit a cigarette, anticipating my protest by saying it would keep the midges away.

'There aren't any yet, it's too cold.'

'Thank you, midge expert Helen.'

'You're welcome, nicotine addict James.'

He plonked a few more pebbles into the placid black

water. Two o'clock and already it was getting gloomy. I wanted to change the mood, make us happy, avoid a row.

'You could film this scene,' I said, 'a remake of *Bad Day at Black Rock*. Or the cod-Gaelic version, *Ochone, Ochone at Dubhsgeir*.' I cackled at my own wobbly joke.

'Possibly. Of course there are no women in that film.'

'We could re-cast ourselves in it. Goodie-with-one-arm Spencer Tracey or baddie-with-cowboy-hat Lee Marvin. Remember that fight scene in the bar?'

Why had I mentioned fight scenes? James stubbed out his cigarette, and flicked another stone into the loch. He was smiling.

'Which do you think I am?'

I examined him theatrically.

'Lee Marvin smoked the way you do. And I'm pretty sure you were born under a wand'rin' star.'

Some people take compliments where none are intended. He laughed quite happily, and the weekend improved. That afternoon I lounged in an armchair reading *The Flight of the Heron*, and James drew a portrait of me. He caught my mood of concentration perfectly, hair falling forward, the frown lines between my eyes. I liked it, he didn't. We propped it on the mantelpiece as we ate supper.

'Thought of a title?' I asked.

'Distance.' He wiped his soup bowl carefully with a crust of bread.

Beyond my kitchen window on the first morning of the new century it has started to rain. Not the soft-scented dampness of the Highlands, but buckets of water chucked violently against the glass. I picture the celebratory crowds in the city centre giggling as they hold jackets over their heads and run for shelter, men dancing in the wet gutters like Gene Kelly. I think about lying in bed in that chilly cottage in Glenfinnan, watching stars flicker through rain in the skylight while James slept.

The portrait has been wrapped in a drawer for nine months. It's still a good drawing, though I no longer think it flatters me. Now I can see what he saw. The distance between us is there in every line.

Perhaps I'd left him, not the other way around. Perhaps his perception had been keener, perhaps to his mind I turned away long before he did. The way he'd said it – 'distance' – not a word he'd searched long and hard to find; on the contrary, an expression of loneliness quietly acknowledged.

I hold the picture up and look at myself next to it in the mirror in the bathroom, and the balance shifts inside me. I feel myself letting go of the story I'd constructed. The goodie and baddie scenario was a protective device that made it possible to go on being right as long as he was wrong. Maybe he wasn't Lee Marvin, and I wasn't Spencer Tracey. Maybe I could rewrite it so we were Bogart and Bergman with bad timing.

With a lump of Blu-tac I stick the portrait up next to the mirror. I make myself smile briefly in contrast to its frown, mutter 'Stupid cow', turn off the light and go to bed. The music next door has stopped. Through the Velux I watch false stars soaring over Edinburgh like fluorescent moths and think of James smoking a cigarette in some other room in some other house in some other city. Before I can change my mind I get out of bed, find a postcard, print his name and address on it and, in the message space, the words: 'Here's looking at you . . . We'll always have Glenfinnan. Happy New Century. Love, Helen.'

It's Good To Talk

'Would you do it again?'

'Yeah, probably. Wouldn't you?'

'I'd like to think I wouldn't have to, you know? But then again, if you're asking me would "I" do it again, if I were the same person in the same circumstances, then obviously, yes, I would, wouldn't I?'

'I suppose so . . .'

'Of course, that's the same kind of arse-numbing pedantry my wife used to complain about. Sorry.'

Michael shrugs away the apology. Patrick offers a cigarette to Michael, but he shakes his head. Michael is eating cashew nuts. He finishes the packet, crumples the foil, and tosses it high into the bare branches of a willow tree. Three small birds take off in alarm. Patrick tut-tuts and resumes.

'I don't think I'd hang myself in the spare room, though. I must have caused Margaret a lot of worry about damage to the roof timbers. Still, it was quick. Not too messy. And she never liked that room anyway.'

Michael shakes his head.

'Well, at least she found you in a couple of hours. If I was going to do it again I wouldn't cut myself in the bath,

I'd drive myself over a cliff or something. Spare everyone the cleaning, you know?'

Patrick picks up a piece of litter from the pathway and puts it in his pocket, nodding.

'Yeah. Sure. Ach, poor Margaret. One of the great clichés, isn't it, my wife doesn't understand me? The way they say it on TV, some pathetic little sod on his knees in front of a young, beautiful woman, saying his wife doesn't understand him, with his hand up her dress . . . it wasn't like that with me at all, it wasn't about sex. She thought it was. And it wasn't that she didn't understand, she just didn't know what to do. She was always watching me, but sort of distant, like if you saw a wild animal with its head in a snare, trying to wriggle its way out? She'd try getting me to hold still, she'd ask me about the noose, she'd ask if it hurt, all that. Quite prophetic. You know? None of it made any difference. They can't really help you.'

Patrick runs his palms across the mark where the rope had bitten into his neck. Unconsciously, Michael traces the scars on the inside of his own forearms, then tucks his hands into his trouser pockets. He sighs, shakes his head.

'I had the same thing with my mother. She was always saying "Ach you'll be fine, you're a big strong fellow." Like I was a sort of Superman, muscles made of Prozac, and I'd never suffer at all because of my size. No emotions because you can lift weights. That suited her, to be the only one with feelings.'

Their walk has taken them some distance already. Michael leaves the path to sit on a wooden bench. Behind him, the leafless trees are dark against a sky which is growing grey and pink. Patrick opens a new pack of cigarettes and lights up. He sits down beside Michael and they gaze at an expanse of water on which bobs a flotilla of miserable-looking ducks.

'Did you try talking to anyone?' asks Patrick.

'Oh yeah. But there was always something – with my mates, they were just going to the pub, or the ex-girlfriend, her new boyfriend was there, or for my mother it was bingo night. Anyway, you know yourself it's bloody hard to phone up and say you want to top yourself, just like that. Who'd listen?'

'I know.'

'I called the Samaritans once. The man on the other end, he was dead young and I started thinking, this is stupid, I know why I'm phoning, I know what's wrong with me, and I don't want this prick trying to talk me out of it, what does he know. It made me angry. And I felt I was doing his head in, too, somebody I didn't even know who was trying to be kind, a volunteer. Imagine how depressing it must have been for him.'

Michael takes a packet of mints out of his pocket, offers it to Patrick.

Patrick takes one and pops it into his mouth, as he grinds out his cigarette. Michael continues, 'And another thing I couldn't get out of my head, when I was lying there in the bath, the way people say "Oh, it's the ones who don't talk about it you really have to watch out for".'

'I know, such an excuse for their own failings . . .'

'Lack of perception, yeah?'

'Stupid bastards . . .'

'I mean, damned if you do talk and damned if you don't. What a choice there.'

They both laugh. The sky grows darker. At the edge of the pond, a slight figure in jeans and a raincoat throws bread to the ducks, which squabble noisily over the manna. Patrick says, 'Did you leave a note?'

'Just the usual, sorry I can't go on, sort of thing. Did you?'

'It was too hard, I kept tearing them up. And there's the other thing, the guilt conflict, you know, where you feel bad enough that you can't go on, but you feel equally bad about giving everyone and their bloody dog the perfect excuse to be pissed off at you. Because you know they're not suddenly going to accept it, you know they'll talk about your selfishness and cowardice, and then how the cheque in the post the next week would have made a difference, or how the footie team won that weekend and how happy you'd have been if only you'd known.'

'And they'll never ever forgive you . . .'

'So you're a complete bastard either way.'

'Failure One or Failure Two.'

'Exactly! You can't win.'

They both laugh.

'It's odd the way we talk about it, like "winners" and "losers", isn't it? Sounds like Tammy Wynette and a man with a gambling problem. D'you think this conversation we're having is at all influenced by the lyrics of country music, Patrick?'

'Or Elvis, maybe. Or Abba. Surely there's been a musical on the subject, that Lloyd Webber man, wasn't there?'

'No, I think he missed that one.'

'Shame. Mind you, he's no talent for comedy.'

'*Suicide – The Musical*. That's more of a Mel Brooks movie, don't you think?'

'Tough job writing the lyrics for it. How do you rhyme overdose or amitryptiline . . .'

'Ah! Something something verbose, something something Abilene?'

'There, now, you see, you have a talent. You could've been Tim Rice.'

'I could have been a contender . . . I coulda been . . . somebody . . .'

Michael laughs at his own Brando parody, which he thinks is pretty good. Patrick runs his hands through his hair, stretches his arms, shakes his shoulders and yawns. A breeze riffles the surface of the water.

'Tiring all this fresh air and analysis, isn't it?'

'It is. Hindsight is a wonderful thing in small doses.'

'Must be supper time by now.'

'Big plate of stew and tatties in front of the fire, couple of hours of TV, warm bath, warm bed, good book . . .'

'I wish.'

'Do you miss it?'

'What . . . life?'

'Mmm.'

They look out at the pond where, in the last of the light, they can watch the ducks waddling slowly up the bank into the undergrowth.

'Not much. Not my actual life. Do you?'

'Sometimes.'

'I don't.'

'There were some good bits, surely?'

'Oh, sure. But they were so long ago. And the good bits were like being a kid and getting a toffee from a stranger – you get suspicious after a while about what the toffee is meant to make you accept.'

'All the shite.'

'Exactly. Exactly that. There is one thing I regret, though.

I'd like to have had a slogan t-shirt made up to wear when I did it.'

'And what would the slogan have been?'

'Nihilism Sucks – It's A Depressives' Thing.'

'Nice one. That would have sold like hot cakes at euthanasia conventions . . . always wondered if old people got confused by Exit signs in big buildings . . . did I tell you I had a career in advertising?'

'Jesus! Pity we never got together back then, we could have made a fortune and died rich.'

'They still wouldn't understand us or forgive us.'

'No. But they'd be crying all the way to the bank.'

Michael gets up. He holds out his hand to Patrick, who takes it and comes to his feet smiling. Behind him, the plaque on the bench reads 'Take Comfort, Weary Traveller'. Patrick swings his arm round Michael's shoulder and they walk slowly up the hill to the gates.

Under Observation

I'm sitting in an airless office. The fan blows floral air freshener in sweeps around the room and nauseates me. The plastic flowers on the desk are swathed in dust and cobwebs. If I blow my nose will they realise it's my allergy, or suspect remorse?

When she brought me in I felt claustrophobic and asked her to leave the door ajar. I have to assert my personality, not behave like a victim. I have to keep thinking. My mind is numb and racing at the same time. I nearly cried when she asked me why I did it. I just managed to say 'I don't know', because what else could I say? She asked, 'Are you having some problems?' I nodded, half kidding, half in earnest. 'I can't . . . I don't want to tell you a sob story.'

She straightens her desk for the sixth time. The pencils in a row, next to the notebook she took from her bag, the box of tissues pushed to the edge nearest me. The notebook's straight edges are aligned with the desk calendar; the phone is absolutely balanced by the position of the out-tray. The mind of an honest person, afraid of corruption.

She called a colleague, a young man in short sleeves and a striped tie. He came in, she went out, we sat in silence.

I asked if this was part of his job, babysitting felons? 'Yeah, s'pose so.' He bit his hangnails till she came back. Waiting for the police to show up, I've been audience to shop gossip. Someone in China is involved with someone else in Cutlery, but her husband is a plumber. Christmas takings look good for this year. Not for me, they don't.

After a while, I feel indignant. They're here because of me, but they're ignoring me. I wait for a pause in their conversation to ask to make a phonecall. Tom isn't in, so I speak blandly to his answering machine. Standing up I can't help but dominate the situation. When I sit down they immediately begin again with staff intrigues. It's bad manners to talk shop in front of guests.

While she's minding me, who's minding the shop? She's probably the boss of a small team, one to a floor, maybe. I admire her shoes. Fourth floor, staff discount. I wonder what she gets paid? If I had a well-paid job would I still nick stuff? She's a human being, at least. Doing her job. I don't resent her. Wonder Boy, though, he's too young to look me in the eye. He wears a signet ring on his pinkie and keeps his nails too long.

Why did I come here today? Why did I get caught, today? There's a lesson in this – don't go shoplifting when your mind's elsewhere. I've never been clumsy before, reckless, yes, but never clumsy. My radar must be jammed. I felt I was being watched and shrugged it off. Stupid.

Nobody followed me down the escalator, or round the make-up counters when I was doing my casual meandering towards the side door, fingering scarves, using the perfume testers. I felt nervous, but not as nervous as I have done. I cleared the door, looked left and right, strolled across the street to the bus stop, sat down.

When she came across the street, she smiled, and I recognised her from the shop, she'd been browsing through knitwear right beside me for a while, just another woman escaping housework. I looked away, back, and then she was inside the shelter.

'Would you come back to the shop please?'

I should have laughed and said, 'No, I'm waiting for a bus'; I should have got up and left. I should have been in another shop, off the street.

But I just sat there, stunned. I said, 'I'm sorry . . . I don't know what you mean.'

'I think you do. You have an item in your bag you haven't paid for, and I'd like you to accompany me back to the shop.'

Our eyes were locked, but I took in all of her, the short blonde hair, the unobtrusive black skirt and jacket, even her shoulder bag looked officially discreet. She seemed confident, and fit enough to run after me, to hold me tight if I struggled. Was she allowed to arrest me? Right here?

I was walking back across the road with her before I knew it – and just as my bus came into view. I moved slowly, trying to assess my chances. Did she have her hand on my arm? Could I take the thing out of my bag without her seeing it?

I throw it in her face, wrenching my arm free of her grip, and she puts one hand up as if to ward off a blow, but the other reaches out for me, catches my collar as I'm turning. I try to unbutton my coat, remember the purse in the left pocket, my driver's licence, keys, and start twisting to get free of her, but she won't let go. The silk has fallen at our feet, she's actually standing on it, as she grabs my arm, and forces it behind my back.

In reality, I did nothing. We went through the back entrance and she asked me to open my bag. I handed over the slithery black wisp. I allowed myself to be marched through the bowels of the store to this stuffy little cupboard.

They're talking about foreign holidays now. They mean Benidorm or villas in Tenerife, not driving through inland Spain or taking night ferries to Rhodes. Safe holidays, meals paid in advance, towels changed twice a week. The Boy Wonder mentions Ibiza, and I snort.

She turns to me then, and apologises for the delay. 'Last time it took an hour for the police to arrive.' I sense a faint but genuine sympathy from her. I wonder if she's ever stolen anything, pencils, bubblegum, as a kid. Perhaps she has children of her own. Will she teach them wrong from right, black and white? In my imagined future I will have children, quick, clever, mischievous. Perhaps I'll dress up like Fagin, and we'll play pickpockets for fun every night before supper. Hysteria creeps up my chest into my mouth and I fight to suppress it.

Mr and Ms Plod eventually stroll in, all black and silver, bursting with the authority the uniform confers. They're my age, in everything but their attitude, their hard faces. Wonder Boy ambles back to his shop floor, and Ms Plod takes the store detective into the corridor to get her statement, leaving me with her partner. He is a great bullock, with the ruddy complexion of a rugby player.

'So, why did you do it?'

Several replies spring to my lips but I can't speak; I'm trembling, I'm choked up, primed to spill great hot tears in front of this smug bastard. I shake my head. He sighs, scratches his chin, and starts to deliver a moral lecture. I'm a silly woman and ought to know better. This sort of thing really doesn't help, etc., etc. Having given the standard speech, he gets more intimate – a one-way intimacy. What do I do? What do I get paid? When did I last work? How often do I do this sort of thing?

'I don't *do* this sort of thing,' I snap back. Oops, watch your temper. But he falls silent.

Ms Plod returns, looks severely at me, cautions me. Have I shoplifted before? Do I have in my possession any other goods for which I have not paid? Choosing to translate the question as 'on my person', I omit to mention the number of Conran garments which lurk in my wardrobe. Funny – my sister quizzed me last week about guilt, after the parcel I sent her, two pairs of trousers and a book on Portuguese cinema which was a bugger to fit into my pocket.

Am I deficient in that area? I feel plenty of guilt about trivial things, like being cool towards someone with thick ankles, not donating to campaigns for better government, eating more chocolate than my waistline can cope with. Not a great legal defence – shoplifting was an alternative to slimming, your honour. The more I ate, the larger a size I was forced to purloin. Ha ha.

I'm asked if I understand what will happen now – I nod, but they explain anyway – a summons, to which I can plead guilty and pay a fine by post or I can contest the charge and go to court. She looks inquiringly at me. The camisole's there, hanging on the back of the door, and I'm stuck here in a corner in my damp raincoat, so why make things more complicated. She nods, satisfied with my attitude, and says I can go.

The store detective is slightly apologetic again as she tells me I'm barred, nevermore to shop in her store. Well, I never bought anything here anyway. I am followed up the back stairs by the male officer. It's stopped raining. I'm aware that he has something to say so I stand there, doing up my coat buttons, looking everywhere but at him. And he surprises me.

'Go home and have a cup of tea. Don't feel too bad about it. It goes on file for seven years, then it'll get wiped. Don't let it ruin your life.' I feel ashamed, then. I just nod a couple of times and walk away, all the way home.

The answering machine shows two messages. Tom. 'Ah . . . I thought you'd be back by now – have you heard any news? Let me know. Bye.' I push *stop*, put the kettle on, take off my coat. I sit down at the desk and push *play* again.

'Just calling to say Mum's all right . . . it was a long operation, but they're happy with it, and she's in Intensive Care, so they'll be keeping an eye on her every minute. I'm going to try to sleep now. Don't worry. I'll call again tonight around six.'

My father's voice is clear all the way from London. Now I can cry.

United Kingdom 1989

Reporting restrictions under the Thatcher government meant that for several years the voices of Gerry Adams MP and other Sinn Fein spokesmen were dubbed by actors.

There's no such thing as a normal Friday evening. Friday is the night for Danny's paper round, then he goes to Cubs, and Iain always comes home late from work, so dinner could be anytime and consequently I am in a mood verging on insubordination. To distract myself from this, I switch on the black and white portable and put it on top of the fridge while I slice vegetables, weeping over the onions and the Channel 4 news. Outside, four floors down, Callum is playing in the garden, a football-pitch sized area resembling Beirut's worst tourist attractions.

Zeinab Badawi levels her gaze at me and reports atrocities, lies and the sins of our fathers. I am trimming cauliflower and keeping an ear open for the latest Irish news when I register screams coming from the communal back garden. I push up the sash and lean out. Callum is biting his nails, standing on one leg and looking up at me; on the ground beside him a girl of about five is bawling her head off. I shout down.

'What's going on Callum?'

'What?'

'I said, what's happened, why's she crying? Is she hurt?'

'Well, I don't know, we were playing with the sticks and she just started crying . . .'

'Did you have a fight?'

By this time, a couple of disembodied heads have joined me at other tenement windows. One, presumably the mother of the now moaning child, starts to yell.

'Amanda, get up off your bottom and come in here *right now!*'

I avoid eye contact, afraid my face will express shock and anger. Callum starts to help the still grizzling Amanda to her feet, brushing down her green tartan skirt.

'Excuse me! Could you ask your wee boy to just leave her alone in the future, please!' Amanda's mother shouts across the length of the garden, and withdraws, banging the window sash down before I have gathered myself to reply in indignation. The other windows close quickly.

Callum looks awkward, forlorn in the empty space. I call more quietly, 'Come upstairs, now.'

'But it wasn't me . . .'

'Yes, well, never mind, we'll talk about it up here, please.'

Callum mutters, kicking at the dry turf. He slouches towards the gate.

The TV is still on in the background, with details of the conflict between warring factions in Belfast, as I return to vigorous action at the chopping board. Suddenly the screen shows two stills under voice-over, Ian Paisley side by side with Gerry Adams. I yell at the set.

'Oh well done! Equally silent for a fucking change!'

Callum trails disconsolately into the kitchen and fingers the mushrooms.

'Hands!'

'Sorry.'

He steps up onto the children's footstool at the sink. I toss onions into a deep pot and stir them around in the hot oil, then lower the heat.

'What's for dinner?'

'Rice and vegetables.'

'Aaaaww . . .'

'Callum . . .'

'Mmm?'

'What was all that about?'

'What?'

'Stop being dense.'

'What? Oh, in the garden?'

'Yes.'

'Amanda's always crying. She just cries to get her own way, and then everyone else gets the blame . . . it's not fair.'

The words sound so adult and composed from the mouth of a seven-year-old, echoing the conversations parents have about other people's children at school gates, in waiting rooms, with husbands and aunts and teachers. But his brow is furrowed and his lips tremble.

Behind us Zeinab pronounces the latest government view on Sinn Fein, the Loyalists, the state of the so-called Union. Peace talks are looking hopeful, she says. I put on water to boil for rice. I dry my hands and sit down, tugging Callum towards me.

'Callum, it's really important for everyone to be treated fairly, but it's also important to tell the truth, isn't it? If you want to be really happy inside, you have to be honest. Hmm? Leave the mushrooms alone, please.'

'Sorry . . .'

'Is that sorry for the mushrooms or sorry for something else, maybe?'

'I didn't do anything else! It was Amanda. I don't like her.'

'Ah. Well. In that case, I'm sorry too. Just keep out of her way, if you don't want to play with her.'

'But it's not fair, is it? I always get the blame, but I'm innocent.'

His use of the expression takes my breath away. I put my hand under his chin so I can see his eyes, which are brimming with tears. I pull him onto my knee and kiss the top of his ear. We sit there, our arms round each other, nibbling at the mound of raw mushrooms until Paisley and Adams quit the screen, and the room is filled with steam and the noise of a kettle furiously boiling.

* * *

It is nine days later, a Sunday night, dark already, and Iain and I have already eaten dinner and are watching TV when the children come back from their mother's house. When we hear their voices in the street, Iain turns off the set and goes to the front door to buzz them into the tenement stair, while I watch from the living room window as they struggle down the pavement carrying bags of school things, shoes, books, clothing. It is the same every other weekend, these miniature treks laden with the possessions from two households, and as always I resent their mother, feel for the children, and detest the whole situation. But I keep out of her way, leave it to Iain to deal with the handover.

Iain's voice carries so well even at a whisper that I can hear his progress down every landing to the bottom. His voice is friendly, but also restrained, as it always is in the presence of his ex-wife. I picture him taking the children's bags under his arms, greeting Danny and Callum and Sophie with kisses, exchanging as few words as possible with Sarah. I picture her at the foot of the stair, clad in clean denim and expensive black leather, car keys in her hand, talking brightly in her brittle voice, goodnights to the children, ostentatiously huge hugs and expressions of love which seem at odds with her normal waspish behaviour.

In fact, I can hear her voice singing out, but the cadence is wrong. Iain's voice drowns her out for a minute, he's shouting something. The children are silent now, no sound of approaching footsteps. Reluctantly, I move towards the flat door, onto the concrete landing in my stocking soles, and look down over the railings.

At the foot of the stair, Sophie has her hand on Danny's shoulder, holding him back. Callum stands higher up, on the turn, looking down, his bag of dirty clothing falling open behind him where he has dropped it. Their attention is on action taking place out of my vision.

I can hear Sarah shout, 'Don't . . . don't you . . . don't you dare!'

I can hear Iain snarl, 'You . . . tell you . . . get out of my sight . . . get out!'

The door slams shut, and then the only sound is of one of the children suddenly crying and the door buzzer being jabbed long and hard by the person outside on the street. Sarah.

I don't go down. I leave Iain to gather his children and their belongings, and shepherd them up. I go back to the window and peer out. A small figure strides back up the pavement to the waiting Citroën, gets in, the brake lights flicker and the car moves away into the light evening traffic.

I watch from the kitchen door as the children arrive in the hall with their father behind them. There's always a strained atmosphere at these times, a period of Cold War, but tonight is more than that. Sophie flicks me a tiny smile, but the whole group is rigid. Iain tells them to dump their bags for tonight and get ready for bed straight away and they don't argue. I follow him into the kitchen where he pulls a carton of apple juice from the fridge and takes deep gulps. Through the thin partition walls I can hear Danny and Callum arguing in their bedroom, and Sophie in the bathroom brushing her teeth. I close the kitchen door and sit down.

'What happened?'

'Oh, well, we had a fight! God, she is a selfish, stupid bitch!'

'Ssh!'

'Well, if they didn't know it already, they ought to know it . . . Jesus!'

'What actually happened?'

'We started arguing, okay, and I told her to leave, and she wouldn't, so I pushed her out the door. Stupid look on her face . . . no, not stupid, smug . . .'

'Oh, for God's sake . . .'

'Stupid bloody bitch, she doesn't give a damn about those kids!'

'Ssh . . .'

I get the cocoa out of the cupboard and start making three half-cups with the remains of the last pint of milk. Iain goes to chase the children towards the bathroom. By the time the cocoa is made and the children are drinking it next to us on the sofa in front of a comedy programme, it is thirty minutes since the incident, and Iain has just about calmed down. Then the main door buzzer sounds. Danny and Callum look at their father and Sophie looks at me, and Iain and I exchange glances. He leaves the room and shuts the door. We can hear him buzzing someone in. He puts his head back round the door and says, 'A couple of cops – she sent the cops round, for God's sake!'

I reach for the remote and hitch the volume up a little. We pretend to watch TV while, in the hallway, Iain assumes his All Men Together voice, but quietly, so that only the tone, a tone which I long to tell him to drop, is heard over the inane prattling and canned laughter from the television. I look down at the faces beside me – Sophie, whose hair I have brushed or plaited most days since she was eight, Danny, whose back I have stroked on nights when his head hurt and he couldn't sleep, and Callum, whose hand is now pressed against my thigh in absent-minded affection and a tacit need for security. I look down at them and see Sarah in their eyes and chins and lips, their small stature. I see Sarah in them and think of the times I have argued with her on the phone about some detail of the complicated weekly schedules. I see Sarah's head turned away from me at every occasion of our chance meeting, and I think about her fluting voice and false values. I see their natural mother in the children's faces and I think of Iain shoving her out of the building in front of them.

The door opens. Iain says, 'Hey guys, these two officers are here to talk about what happened downstairs with your mother. Okay?' His voice is bright with artificial calm.

The uniforms step into the room. They bring the smell

of the night with them, rain and wet leaves, and perhaps instant coffee. They have their caps under their arms, and one of them holds a notebook and pencil. The other one nods at me, and then looks at the children.

'My name's Graham, and this is Steve. Now, we'll just have a wee chat, okay?'

Iain motions me to come out of the room. I frown, but he beckons me. When I reach the door I say to the officer called Graham, 'Are you going to talk to them for long? They're very tired and quite upset . . .'

'. . . just a couple of minutes,' says Iain, interrupting. 'We'll wait in the kitchen. Now guys, you just say what you saw, okay?'

Steve shuts the door behind us. Iain takes my arm and leads me into the kitchen.

'What are you doing?' I ask, in a half whisper. 'Are you bloody mad? You shouldn't let them talk to the police on their own.'

But Iain doesn't answer beyond saying that it will be alright. I know he is wrong. It will never be alright. Never. I look at him sitting at the table, sorting through piles of old letters, parking tickets, children's school reports, avoidance activity. My throat feels tight, fear will not leave me. I move cautiously back towards the living room. I crouch down with my back to the bathroom door, stare at the floorboards and listen.

I can hear Danny saying, 'No, well, Mum was standing at the door, almost in the street, and Dad was like where you are, but it was quite far away . . .'

Callum interrupts, 'He was holding her arm . . .'

Sophie says, 'No, Callum, he wasn't.'

Callum says, 'He was holding Mum's arm . . .'

Danny says, 'And they were shouting a lot, but I didn't really hear what they were saying . . .'

Callum says, 'Because we were crying.'

One of the officers asks something in a voice too low to decipher.

Danny says, 'No, I couldn't really see, but I don't think so.'

Sophie says, 'They were just fighting, I mean arguing . . .'

Callum says, 'Yeah, that's when Dad hit her. When he hit Mum.'

Danny says, 'No he didn't, Callum, you're making it up.'

Sophie says, 'They do argue a lot.'

I get up quietly and go into the bathroom, locking the door behind me. I sit on the edge of the bath in the dark. Soon enough, I hear the living room door open; the two policemen emerge, now laughing with the children, asking them about school and homework. Iain comes into the hall and tells the kids to scoot to bed, now. Then he accompanies the officers to the front door, and onto the landing. Once again, their voices are quiet, but the tone carries well enough. Three men discussing a domestic dispute. The witnesses are minors. The ex-wife will be informed that her charges cannot be substantiated. These things happen. Goodnight, Sir.

Iain comes back into the flat and closes the door. He knocks on the bathroom door.

'You in there?'

'Yes.'

'They've gone.'

'I know.'

'Okay.'

When I hear him go into the living room I flush the

toilet and come out. I say good night in turn to the children. I kiss Callum, and his stuffed dog, and promise to leave the door ajar. I tell Danny the lights are going out in two minutes. In Sophie's room, I tuck her in tight, the way she prefers, and stroke her hair off her face. I recite our ritual of 'Sleep tight, sweet dreams', and she repeats it back to me. Then I go back to Danny, take the book out of his hands, and turn off the lamp. He rolls onto his stomach groaning and says, 'Will you scratch my back?'

I squat down beside his bed and run my fingers over his skin, feeling the rib bones, the muscles; quite a fragile little bird. I make my touch light, and circular, hypnotic. I write his name and then mine across his shoulder blades, and he grunts in recognition. Then I smooth down his t-shirt and tug the duvet over his shoulders and get up and go out, leaving the door ajar as promised.

In the living room, Iain is stretched along the sofa. The *Nine o'Clock News* has just started, but the sound is off, so the armoured cars trundle silently up and down the Falls Road area of Belfast without comment. I stand behind the sofa and look down. His eyes are shut, and his breath is coming in little puffs, his head cushioned in the crook of his right arm. In repose, there is no anger left in his face.

The Sidekick

'Could you . . . just . . . give us a minute? Please?'

'Sure.'

Don got out of the car, hesitated, then closed the door neither softly nor forcefully, leaving Cat alone with Michael. Cat heard Don's cowboy boots scuffing tarmac as he walked round the back of the vehicle, calling to the crew about where he wanted to set up the next shot. All four came into sight, heading towards the airport departure terminal, lugging silver equipment cases, the tripod, the fluffy-covered boom. None of them looked back.

What did they think she was doing? Cat wondered. She didn't know the answer herself, only that her head was too full of anger and frustration to behave civilly, say her lines, hit her mark, smile – any of that was beyond her capacity until she had been in a quiet space for a few moments. She tried to breathe more slowly, relax her body. She looked at the back of Michael's head, wondering why he hadn't got out too. He sat very still in the front seat. The collar of his pale khaki raincoat was askew, and she imagined leaning forward to fold it properly, smooth it flat, but they had never really touched in any intimate way and she couldn't do it now. Then she realised her mistake with Don. She had used the plural – Us. Could you give Me a minute, was what she had intended to say, the Us merely a colloquial slip of the tongue, but now interpreted to indicate something much more important and private.

Michael said nothing. Cat wasn't used to him quiet, half expected a quip.

She remembered watching him for the first time on TV, presenting his usual show, a late-night programme, that week featuring an artist who painted on cardboard spread on the floor with his fingers covered in household emulsion; white, blue, red. Michael, in his cool grey suit, had been urbane, witty and cynical. That was long before she knew they'd be working together, and she'd judged him as potentially arrogant, patronising, certainly not her type. Meeting him had rapidly changed that view. With the first handshake, the first smile, his charm had taken her by surprise. Over the past three weeks she had learned that the charm was genuine, and his interest in her more than purely professional and not in the least paternal.

Yet nothing had actually happened, nothing was said, and they sat together now in a deepening silence which said nothing and everything. The fact that he was in the car with her, waiting for some explanation of 'us', suddenly hit her and she felt sick. She rubbed her hands thoughtlessly through the elaborate new haircut stiff with lacquer.

The last day of filming had separated Cat and Michael for six hours. She had imagined him doing pieces to camera all over the city, making jokes with the crew, meeting actors and dancers and authors, eating some deliciously expensive lunch with Don, while she had been in the smartest salon in the city getting a make-over for a thirty second visual joke destined to go under the end titles. Michael was the important one. He was The Presenter, she was the lowly native sidekick. After she complained apologetically that no-one paid any attention to her suggestions he had explained this succinctly. 'Listen, love, no-one cares what you want because you're a girl.' She was stung by that until she caught his eye. His facial expression clearly indicated the sexual preference of the director, and offered compassion for her naïveté as well as her gender. He had taught her a tough lesson about the need for power, by showing her how little she truly possessed.

Cat hated hairdressers. Hated the salon full of noise and heat, and the punishment of having to watch herself, in the mirrored hell, becoming a puppet in the hands of an egomaniac who wielded sharp implements with frightening authority. The dyeing had taken hours, then cutting, layering, and finally there was the humiliation of having her face painted, by a self-absorbed teenager, to resemble one of the pouting mannequins in the fashion shots which adorned the walls. Her so-newly-fledged ego had fluttered and expired like a nervous canary under hands that fussed and primped. The day had stolen her time and equilibrium and, most important of all, her identity.

Emerging hungry and quietly furious in the late afternoon, she had been shocked to notice the sun low in the sky, to hear Don tell her there was just one more scene to do before Michael caught the plane home to his other life. To his wife and his child.

Perhaps he was gone already, sitting there so still. He might have begun the reverse transition to husband and father while she craned her neck for the scissors, submitted to the enamelling of her skin. She was overtaken by a terrible panic, like a child dressed up in play clothes, tugging an adult's arm, asking for a sweet little piece of attention. Give 'Us' a minute. Please.

Cat imagined Michael's face betraying impatience, contempt, now that it was hidden from her, now that he was about to leave. She delved into the pocket of her coat for the envelope with his name on it and held it cautiously, pondering the new significance of its contents.

The first couple of days on the series had been crazy, no time to think, no idea what she was doing, simply spouting the lines the director fed her and adding her own touch to the delivery, exhausted at the end of each day by all she had learned. By the end of week one, her confidence had taken a leap, and she'd looked to the director and producer for some sign that she was doing a good job, but none came. She hadn't been yelled at, told her contract was cancelled, that they'd found somebody else, so clearly they were reasonably satisfied. Nevertheless her stomach knotted every morning on the train to work and she dreamt of failure every night.

After the fifth day of filming, Cat and Michael had waited in a chic restaurant for an hour until joined belatedly by Don and a young man who, it became apparent from their discussion about an imminent Italian holiday, was Don's boyfriend. That pre-dinner hour together had afforded them their first personal conversation. As they consumed garlic bread and olives, Michael talked about his early years as an interviewer, meeting prime ministers, pop stars, movie idols, with a nonchalance that impressed Cat more than she cared to acknowledge. Then he encouraged her to talk, interviewed her. Did you go to drama school? Where? What was it like? Tell me about how you got your break. What do you think about television? 'I like your work on this, by the way,' he said casually, sipping Côtes du Rhône. She had looked down at her plate and hoped she was not blushing, looked back up and caught the gleam of his teeth in a grin that recognised her predicament, and a tacit intimacy was established.

Michael's head was turned slightly to follow the incoming path of a small jet. The silence in the car grew enormous, and she challenged it with a gesture, holding the envelope over his shoulder so that he saw it from the corner of his eye. He reached up and took it.

'Should I open it now?'

'Keep it for the plane.'

'OK. Ready to go and do it?' His hand on the door handle.

'I suppose so.'

Without waiting for her, Michael climbed out of the car, flicking the lock, and set off across the tarmac towards Don and the crew who, it now appeared to Cat, were waiting with a sort of assumed resignation that gave her a fresh burst of indignant temper, her baby ego fighting back. She slammed her own door and walked across to her position in front of the camera, head up.

The last scene was simple, a one-take job which she got through with her fists clenched and then, in a flurry, the crew were packing up, Don was shaking Michael by the hand, and Michael had kissed her cheek, waved a general goodbye, and rushed to catch the shuttle flight. Cat walked with Don back to the car while he talked on the mobile. She felt bewildered and empty. They drove in conversational vacuum back to the studios, took the lift two floors up, strode past the glossy showbiz pictures that lined the corridor to the production offices. Don excused himself, and Cat wandered around in the reception area, unsure what was expected of her. Should she go home, say good-bye, thank someone? A researcher glanced at her in passing, acknowledged her presence with a fractional lifting of the chin, which Cat returned with a false smile, conscious only of her tension.

Through the glass wall of an office down the corridor she could hear the murmur of voices, one of them familiar but out of place. She walked towards it, knocked and went in. Her agent was standing next to the producer, and both looked pleased to see her hovering at the door. Joanne, rustling in orange silk, slithered across the room on dancer's legs to give Cat a theatrical hug and kiss. Her voice was pure Joan Greenwood, tempered by Leith and Silk Cut, and she oozed sincerity.

'Ooh, your hair! Wonderful! Super make up . . . Darling, you should do your face like that more often! Doesn't she look fantastic, Adrian? Did you get any stills, love? Adrian, I hope you're going to put my young lady up on your wall of fame?'

Until then Cat had almost forgotten the transformation of her physical appearance from ingénue to sophisticate. She excused herself and rushed to the ladies'. Against the surrounding monotony of cream tiles, the reflection in the mirror showed her a composed, attractively slender young woman, hair streaked with red and pink and amber, eyes made emphatic by black and blue shadows, mouth outlined in garish magenta. It was a face from a magazine cover, nobody she recognised or would ever want to meet again. Her agent loved her like that, and Michael – he hadn't commented.

Tears left streaky tracks down her powdered face. She used wet paper towels and hand soap to scrub away at the muck until her skin was clean, dragged wet fingers through her hair until it was tangled and unglamorous, so that she looked like a child, as young and insignificant as recent experience had shown her to be. Retrieving her coat and bag, she headed for a discreet fire exit staircase down to the car park, and walked quickly, head down, to the station.

On the train she took an airline seat, back to the engine, and kept her eyes closed, replaying scenes from the past three weeks. Michael nudging her foot under the table during a short scene in which she was trying to sound serious. Herself cracking up at the faces he pulled during reverses. The memory of successfully improvised dialogue in a courtyard full of onlookers. The warmth of his eyes on her face when she was talking to camera. Finally, she let herself remember the worst and the best.

On the penultimate day Don had seemed more relaxed, almost chatty. During a break when they were waiting for the crew to strike the lights, and Michael had gone off to use a phone, she'd been seduced into talking more personally, and made some reference to Michael as a God-like figure in the world of television. Don gave her an odd look and said incredulously, 'Well, yes, but surely you must know he's in love with you?' Her apparent confusion clearly entertained him. She pretended to laugh it off but was haunted by the remark, by the possibility that it was more than a cruel piece of teasing. Until then she had been drifting unconsciously from one day to another without considering what would happen next, aware only of her good fortune in having the job, and of a growing affection for Michael. In the immediate aftermath of Don's remark, Cat experienced the terrifying sensation of travelling at speed in one direction while looking resolutely backwards, watching opportunity rush past out of her reach. Her high moral beliefs about adultery took a severe jolt, and she almost cried aloud with the sudden awareness of wanting Michael, hoping with ferocity that Don's remark had been the truth and simultaneously that it had not.

She opened her eyes as the train slowed. They were coming to a station and passengers exchanged places. She thought about Michael hailing a taxi and being driven homewards, eager to see his family. She wondered if he had opened the envelope, what his reaction had been to the small gift, the carefully chosen words on the card. She saw again the back of his head in the car, the collar of his rain-coat, imagined him turning round, speaking to her, some remark that would soothe, explain, encompass all that had not happened and make it less devastating. She knew that her foolish 'Us' had compromised him in some way that could hardly be called professional. The more she ran the scene in her mind, the less likely it seemed to her that she would ever hear from him again.

During the following week life resumed its dull sheen of normality. She talked with her agent about projects, meet-ings, future possibilities. Don sent her a perfectly pleasant letter in which he thanked her for taking part in the series and made no mention of her diva-like behaviour on the last day. The fee came through. She caught up on sleep. She trimmed her hair with nail scissors to make it her own again. All the time she was consciously avoiding thinking about Michael she thought about him anyway.

The next broadcast of his usual programme was buried in late-night scheduling, the date ringed in red felt-tip in her diary. On the night, she sat upright on the sofa, glass of water in one hand, remote in the other, until the opening credits, then leaned forward, brought up the volume. There he was. There he was. Hands behind his back, in the centre of a dark studio. He wore another light grey unstructured suit without a tie, his trademark. He began talking quietly about the subjects to be covered in the next thirty minutes.

As the camera slowly moved to a tight head shot she saw what she'd been warning herself not to hope for, telling herself not to expect. A little piece of metal glinted on the lapel of his jacket. Turned sideways, so it no longer looked kitsch or phallic, lay a tiny space-rocket pin. The silver shimmered against the fabric with subtle intent. When the camera was close enough for her to see his eyes, she shuffled closer to the screen, and then she knew absolutely that they were talking to each other. Never mind the words on the autocue, never mind the wider audience of insomniacs and shift workers and lonely singles, she knew his smile was for her, that he was saying, 'Hello, Cat.' She put her hand to his face on the screen and felt the electricity crackle, and her own face became a smile so huge and fierce it hurt her jaws.

Xmouse

My grandmother had a pair of old-fashioned brass light fittings. They were gooseneck-shaped, actually three baby goosenecks sprouting from each oval base, topped by pleated shades of red nylon with darker red tassels. In all the years I went to visit Gran and sat in her front room I never saw those lights switched off until the day she went into hospital. Then, going round her house early that morning, checking all the plugs were out of sockets, pulling the curtains away from the radiators, I noticed the dust, especially on the lamps. Thick ropes of grey felt along the top of the shades, specks clinging like dandruff to the tassels, and inside, where the bulbs were yellowed, fur so thick hardly any light could squeeze out.

I remembered all that in one sharp flash; Gran peering at her magazines in the terrible light, shifting her glasses to see the crossword clues, while I was standing in B&Q, in an aisle between Electrical and Homewares, looking for a mousetrap. Right in front of me were identical lamps, same shades even, but all clean and shiny and priced at £34.99 the pair (excluding flex). And I wondered if Gran's lamps were still up on the walls of that bungalow, energy-efficient bulbs shining through new shades onto some other old lady's gleaming coal scuttle and polished fire tongs.

But wondering doesn't get jobs done, and I knew I was just wasting time dreaming about the past so I didn't have to make a decision about the mousetrap. Gran never had mice in that house because Hector chased them away. Hector was her cat, a heavy white animal with a pink and black nose and pale eyes. Gran inherited him from a bingo friend who'd died: a sizeable inheritance. I don't think he ever caught any mice, just deterred them. Not difficult, his breath was enough to make your eyes water. He patrolled his new home like a tough guard at a high security prison, just waiting for a rodent to step out of line. If Hector had been human he'd have been an unrepentant bully, and if he'd been there in B&Q standing next to me, he'd have whispered in my ear, 'What's your problem, pal? Too bloody namby-pamby to get rid of vermin, ya tosser? Here, forget these wee one-at-a-time dodges, get a big box of poison, that's your problem solved. Get on wi' it!'

But Hector's dead, the smelly bastard, buried in Gran's garden, and maybe I am a namby-pamby tosser, but I've never knowingly harmed a living creature in my life. Wandering through Macho Man World was a mistake.

The first dropping appeared at the start of December. I wondered if it could be a bit of leaf tea, and then I thought: Derek, you daft sod, when's the last time you used anything except a bloody teabag – right, never. After that I found a few more every morning, mostly in the kitchen. They weren't on the counter tops, so I made myself ignore the situation, just cleaned up a bit better, though, having said that, I haven't looked behind the fridge or the stove since

I moved in here and I really, really do not want to 'cause it'd probably turn my stomach. I genuinely forgot for a few days, but then I opened my food cupboard and saw frilly-edged holes chewed in a bag of rice, the flour, the lentils, even a box of matches had one of its corners gnawed away, and little black commas lay scattered everywhere. I felt a coldness in my guts, like when I was fourteen and discovered that some boys down the street had rubbed dogshit on the saddle and handlebars of my new bike.

I chucked everything that wasn't in jars or cans into the bin, and got a rag and bleach and cleaned the cupboard and all that was left in it, and then tried to work out where the wee bugger had invaded. There was no gap that looked wide enough even for a beetle. From then on I kept the cupboard doors closed really tight but still, somehow, every day there'd be a few more curls of dung on the shelves. Calling cards of poop.

I didn't say a word about it to Aileen, my girlfriend, because she's a total neat-freak. Aileen works in a solicitor's office. It's the perfect job for an insecure person; all about rules, so as long as you've done everything right no-one can touch you. If you have clean hair, wear the same sort of clothes as the other secretaries, eat the same low-fat lunches, share the same nail-buffing fetish, fancy the same pop stars, and if you're the only person who knows how to order stationery and fix the coffee machine, then, even if your boss is earning eight times your salary and lives in a massive country house and gets monumentally crabby when he forgets his indigestion tablets, your ego stays pretty bouncy. That's the way I look at it, but I've never shared my analysis with Aileen.

I like Aileen mainly for things she doesn't even know

about. Her smiles when she wants to get her own way, heart-stoppers, even though they're pure manipulation. The way she nibbles an apple right down to the stalk. The shape of her back when she's sitting at her desk, feet tucked under her chair, showing the pale soles of her high-heeled boots. Her pleasure in music and dancing. Most of all I like the look of her first thing in the morning, her clean eyelashes so gold-red against her freckled skin. First time I saw that, the morning after our third date, my heart turned over.

Her one major flaw is her phobia about mess. She prefers to spend our times together either out in a restaurant or a cinema, or at friends' houses, or at her place, where she is in control since her flatmate is rarely at home. Aileen likes to sleep in her own bed in her own very tidy bedroom in her own very modern flat, on a soft mattress covered in crisp lilac sheets, with novels and tubes of hand cream nicely organised on her night-table, and red velvet clogs tucked side by side under the valance. I don't have a valance on my bed, and if I did, and she looked under it, she'd probably find something to complain about. Dust, or mouse droppings, I mean, nothing sinister. I tend to do a quick dash round with the dustbuster before she visits, just so I can relax. I do really like her, she's lovely and quite clever and funny, but there've been hints dropped about the cost of two rents and ideal places to hold wedding receptions so much recently it's beginning to get on my nerves. I like living alone, it suits me.

Two weeks before Christmas, however, I finally met my new, uninvited flatmate. I was in the living room slumped in a chair watching TV, and I reached my hand down to the floor for my coffee mug and nearly tipped it over 'cause I was laughing at the time – something American on

Channel 4 – so I looked down to see if I'd spilt any liquid and saw a grey shape move across the fireplace. So small it could have curled up in a walnut shell. It didn't scuttle, but it didn't creep along either, it had quite a purposeful pace. Maybe it didn't see me, because I barely moved a muscle, except for my hand which found its way to the mug and lifted it onto my stomach as if the floor wasn't safe any more – but the mug slipped and sloshed and I jumped up and cursed at the soggy, burning feeling as coffee dripped all down my shirt and jeans. And when I looked back to the fireplace, of course, the mouse had vamoosed.

I crawled around, scouting under furniture for mouse-sized gaps. You read about big game hunters looking for pawprints, and I pictured myself as an urban Hemingway, stalking with patience and respect for the cunning of my prey. There would be no easy-to-spot trail of indentations across damp river mud, but something like flour could work. I'd binned the flour though, so I found some talcum powder, an unwanted gift. It had a musky scent I didn't much like, and I wondered if the mouse would turn up its nose at the pong, but it was worth a try. It went down in fine sprinkles and I smoothed it out carefully with the back of a wooden spoon so there was a thin, even coating near the gaps in the floor and skirting, and a long drift across the hearth. The whole flat stank, but I was proud of my ingenuity.

Later, reading in bed, I found my attention slipping. Instead of following the book's plot – the sexual adventures of some world-weary photographer in LA – my mind skipped between Aileen and the mouse. Thoughts of Aileen provoked a bit of anxiety, the mouse mainly curiosity, but when I thought of them both together I felt slightly sick.

There was a hovering, ticklish wobble in my chest, a mixture of fear and excitement, like when you're young and stupid and take drugs you've never tried before from someone you hardly know, and only then wonder what could happen in the next five seconds, ten minutes, rest of your life.

For the next week I checked my talcum traps every day for signs of activity, but there was nothing, no pawprints, no new chew marks. Then, one suppertime, I opened a kitchen cupboard and peered in for inspiration, and a tiny face peered back at me from behind the lime marmalade.

The mouse sat very, very still. I whispered, 'It's all right, it's okay, don't panic.' I could have been talking to myself as much as to the mouse, we'd both had a real scare. I kept gazing at the tiny thing, its glossy black eyes, the shape of its nose, the minuscule digits on its long pink feet. The pelt was a greenish grey, almost licheny, a colour I've never really seen before, and nothing like the hair of older women despite the expression.

I was bent over, half squatting, so my knees were complaining and behind me on the stove the water was boiling away ready for pasta, and half my brain was thinking, hurry, catch it, and the other half was going, Derek, you dope, shut the door, come back in two minutes and it'll be gone. Before I'd consciously chosen an option I'd closed the door and left the kitchen, and when I came back and looked again, muscles tense in case of another surprise, the cupboard was bare. Well, mouse-free. No way to tell where it had come from or how it had sneaked out, no Mouse Friday marks on the floors at all. After supper I vacuumed up all the talc.

The weather got very cold and I bought a new scarf for myself, green and blue stripes, and one for Aileen, hot colours, pink and red lambswool with little bobbles on the ends, which I wrapped up for her Christmas present. We'd planned to spend Christmas Eve together before she went to her family in Fife. On the afternoon of the 24th I came home a bit early from work and started making dinner. This time, when I opened the cupboard for a jar of curry paste, the mouse was on a different shelf, half hidden among the spare cups and old flower vases from Gran's house. I went 'Woah!' – not a yell, or a scream, just a weird startled noise. I didn't move and neither did the mouse, but I quickly looked around and spied a glass measuring jug near the sink, and got hold of that. The mouse must have been watching my eyes, waiting for its chance, because he suddenly made a run for it, scrabbling along the shelf, dodging past cans of corn and tuna, launching into the air onto the chrome kitchen stool, then another huge leap down onto the floor by my foot and just as it landed, with a teeny plopping noise – and without even thinking about co-ordination – I plonked the jug down over it. My legs were shaking at the speed and the fluke of trapping it at all, so I kept my hand on the base of the jug and knelt down on the lino for a closer look. I could see the wee beast freeze as it realised its escape bid had been ruined. It was a bit like *The Great Escape*, the scene with Steve McQueen when his stolen motorbike piles into a barbed wire barricade, and he's almost smiling as he tries to put his hands up. Putting a brave face on defeat. At that moment I felt so sad, almost ashamed of having caught this mouse, that I nearly lifted the jug. I was stopped by a knock at the front door.

It was one of my neighbours with a cheap card and a few slightly inebriated words on his love of the festive season. He kept me there for maybe ten minutes reciting his favourite Gordon Ramsay recipe for stuffed turkey drumsticks. I was finally getting the conversation wound up when in off the street and up the stair in a rush came a pink-cheeked Aileen. We had a quick introduction and recap on turkey serving suggestions, and then I got the door closed and gave Aileen a big hug which she, fuelled by claret at her office party, quite ardently turned into something else.

It's a sign of how much I like Aileen that I entirely forgot about the mouse problem for at least twenty minutes until I got a sudden image of the poor creature imprisoned in his airless space, gasping like a mime artist with asthma. I pulled on my jeans and was halfway out the bedroom door when Aileen said, 'Where are you going, mister, come back here . . .' and I stopped, buttoning my fly, and said, 'Er, fancy a glass of wine?' and she flicked her hair out of her eyes and said, 'Mmmmmmmhhhmmmm' in a really feline way, which normally would have had me rushing back to her but right then just made me weirdly nervous.

He was okay, still breathing. I grabbed a takeaway menu and lifted the jug a fraction, and started sliding one under the other. He retreated in a rapid shuffle till he'd gone full circle and was crouched over the Szechuan banquet options. Slowly, I turned the jug over, felt his weight shift and heard his toenails scritch against the glass, and then the jug was on the counter right way up, swiftly topped by a soup bowl. Immediately I started looking for something bigger to house him, until tomorrow, when Aileen would be gone. My plastic mop bucket was almost brand new and not too scummy. I didn't want him getting chemicals on his paws and then his whiskers dropping out when he cleaned himself. So I tipped him in at an angle, the way you pour bottled beer into a glass, and lowered a slice of carrot in beside him, and laid a dishcloth over the top, and put the bucket out of sight in the nook by the washing machine. Only just in time, because Aileen came slinking in wearing nothing but my bath towel. She snuggled up behind me and said, 'I'm hungry, Derek', in a tired wee girl voice, and I had to turn my attentions to cooking.

Around eleven on Christmas Day morning I walked Aileen to her bus stop. She was wearing her new scarf and a pair of Jackie O sunglasses for her hangover, and with her red hair hanging loose round her, breath turning to fog in the chill, she looked great. But as soon as she was on the bus and out of waving distance I jogged back home to Steve. The mouse. Like Steve McQueen, in his cooler. Well, I had to call him something. He wasn't anonymous any more, not to me.

Steve had munched some carrot and left a few turds on the bottom of the bucket. The face and body language of such a small animal don't give much away, so I didn't know if he'd had any sleep, or been frantic and exhausted all night trying to jump out. I sat on the kitchen floor and tried to think what to do for him. If I let him go, we'd be back to square one. If I released him in the garden he'd probably get caught by a bird or a cat, or freeze to death, or be beaten up by gangs of bigger mice for stepping into their territory. The fact was, he was a house mouse who belonged in a house. Just not mine. I wondered if there was another house he could live in, if I ought to post him through the letterbox of some grand place with lots of rooms where he'd have a happier life. Then I began to ask myself if somewhere under my floor Steve had friends, maybe a family, who'd be missing him. He could be a daddy with wee mouths to feed. It was all a bit depressing.

So I called the SSPCA. Of course, being Christmas, there was just an answering machine, but it gave an emergency number and I tried that and left mine and a while later, when I was in the bath, I got a call back.

She sounded young, and she was already impatient. I started to explain the basics but when I mentioned the word mouse she snapped, 'Is it a pet?' 'No,' I said, 'it's wild, but domestic, if you know what I mean.' 'So it's not a fancy mouse?' she demanded, and again I said, 'No, not tame, just an ordinary grey mouse, not piebald, doesn't do tricks.' She snorted, 'Just let it go then,' like I was a halfwit, and I began to say why I'd already ruled that out, but she said, 'Look, I can't help you. Just let it go.' I told her I'd expected more compassion from an animal-loving organisation, that if it was a horse or a dog she wouldn't be so casual, and wasn't she sidestepping the real issues, but she half-yelled something about 'I've got six sheep on a frozen pond to worry about today, so you'll have to work this out for yourself', and put the phone down. A disappointingly unprofessional attitude.

What's the big difference between a sheep and a mouse? Obviously, the sheep is bigger and fluffier and has an owner, so in the eyes of most people it's valued more highly than, say, a small wild thing, a creature you can't keep in flocks and shear for fleece and herd into trucks to the abattoir. Isn't it unfair and a bit creepy if you're nicer to one animal than to another because of the way it tastes after you've killed it? I'll admit I like eating sheep myself, but the point remains valid.

I gave Steve a corner of my leftover breakfast croissant and carried him in his bucket into the living room. I flicked on the telly and there, spooky but predictable, was the classic Christmas Day family movie – *The Great Escape*. Why do they do it? It's a really sad film. Most of the escapers get shot in the end, not exactly a cheery message of good-will to all men and hope and joy to the world. Still, once it had started I had to watch and I got drawn into the story all over again, totally gripped, especially near the end when Steve's character is roaring along the side of that hill, trying to get enough height to jump the massive, cruel fences. He makes it over the first one, but the soldiers are closing in, and he builds up speed and tries the next, and his bike soars off the ground but not enough, not enough, and he goes crashing down into the vicious roll of spiked wire, the bike flips over, and he is caught, lying there, all tangled up, just waiting to be hauled back to the concentration camp, back to his dark, solitary cell. The Cooler King.

If Aileen had been there she'd have cried her heart out and I wouldn't have; but because she wasn't, I did. When the end credits rolled I'd used up seven tissues, and after I'd finished sobbing like a baby I knew my sadness was because now that I had him, I wanted to set Steve free.

I took him to the cupboard in the kitchen. I opened the door, and moved stuff around so I could put the bucket in, propped on its side a bit so he could walk up and jump out with no problems. I didn't say a word, just got up, took my jacket and scarf and keys and went out for a walk. And when I got back he was gone. I drank four glasses of wine and fell asleep on the sofa.

On the 27th I went round to Aileen's. I knew she'd be keen to spend the day scouring the sales with me in tow, which I hate, and as soon as I arrived and saw the set of her face I could feel a row brewing. After an hour of being lectured on my antisocial, unromantic, impossible personality, I said I'd had enough and was going home, and she said, 'Fine', and folded her arms and wouldn't look at me. Ten minutes later, striding along like a sulky teenager, I realised her family must have been grilling her about me, whether we had a future together and all that rubbish, prodding all her insecurities, and that I was probably edgy and dull company because I was preoccupied with thoughts of justice and freedom and principles. I could have gone back and apologised, but I didn't know if I could spend more hours of my life with someone who cared so much about petty stuff like hair clips and shiny shoes and valances.

I body-swerved the busy shopping streets and walked through residential bits of town, looking at other people's lives through glass. Highly decorated Christmas trees, mantels and windowsills lined with cards showing robins and snowmen. Holly wreaths on the smart doors and next to them bin-bags stuffed with garish wrapping paper. Families together, adults lying on carpets playing with their kids' new games, kids in front of the box, blue light flooding their pasty faces. All the domestic bliss you can buy. I felt envious and cynical at the same time.

It was getting dark and I was hungry, but I went on walking, past the railway station, past the big brewery, along the canal path and out to where I could see hills dusted with snow. That's where I found a B&Q and got sucked into it, loud and bright and busy with harried-looking couples pushing trolleys full of tiles and garden furniture and paint testers. And that's where I had my existential moment in front of the lamps that reminded me of Gran and her nasty second-hand cat and my big dilemma.

Pest Control was in the same aisle as the weedkiller, unsurprisingly. The shelves were stacked with bottles and packets labelled Death, Danger, Toxic, and just to take the edge off the fear, Bargain Prices. Down in the clutter at floor level I spotted a few flimsy cardboard boxes the size of fag packets, and picked one up. On the cover in black and red was a cartoon sketch of a smiling mouse, its whiskers curved like an upside down handlebar moustache. A schizophrenic rodent, happy to be caught? A horrible piece of design. I opened the box and examined the fatal device. It had a cheap wooden base, a copper-coloured wire spring, a latch to hold the mechanism in place, a sharp bit where you were supposed to shove an enticing cube of Cheddar. I imagined myself putting some toast on the spike, setting the spring, leaving it in the cupboard; I let myself hear the vicious snap it would make in the middle of the night if it functioned as directed. Nope. Couldn't do it. I dropped it back on the shelf. If I wanted the mouse out of my house, I'd find a different way.

Back at my place, I checked Steve's favourite cupboard. No friendly face peeking back at me, but clues to his presence lay scattered around the tins, and he'd nibbled the corners of a tomato soup label. Bad Steve. I went into my junk cupboard and rummaged around for a bit. On the way home I'd had a slightly weird idea for a humane method of capture, a Heath Robinson-type thing, and I was pretty sure I could rig it up. I found a clear plastic shirt box and some white thread and a bit of thin dowelling and took them to the living room table to assemble. The phone rang twice, but I left it; I could tell from the timing that it would be Aileen, she tends to call during the ad breaks of the soaps. She didn't leave a message, though, and I felt a bit guilty, but also quite relieved. I was enjoying my craft project. I punched a few holes in the plastic box for air, and got it propped up with a six-inch piece of dowel sunk into a lump of Blu-tac so it wouldn't skid. Then, using a button for bait, I pretended my finger was a small sensitive nose looking for nice things to eat, nudging the pearly button so that the thread it was attached to tugged at the dowel and the almost invisible box came down with a light clunk. Not as noble and grand as the Hemingway method, or as sneaky as a native pit lined with stakes, but it would do the job.

I reassembled it on the floor in the darkest corner of my living room, moving a chair so I could keep it in view from the sofa. I substituted a heel of bread smeared with peanut butter for the stand-in button, and did another test, and then I made myself a cheese sandwich and a pot of tea and turned off all the lights in the living room except a single reading lamp, and sat on the sofa with my book. I tried to read, but the plot failed to absorb me. I found my eyes going to the corner again and again, which reminded me of Gran's favourite saying about watched pots. So I sat and looked at the mousetrap and let my mind wander in the half dark.

Soon, I was away in the past, aged thirteen, one of many evenings spent in Gran's front room. The red-shaded lamps cast little halos of sickly orange light over us as we sat side by side on her old sofa. I could almost feel the texture of the stretchy nylon cover over the lumpy seat. The room was too hot, all three bars of the electric fire glowing in the hearth. Gran had one foot up on a padded stool, resting her bad ankle, and in her lap was a copy of the local paper, folded open to the TV guide. On the box, a hatchet-faced man in a tight suit held a microphone under the nose of a giggling Essex housewife. I remembered the jazzy theme tune, how I'd been bored by the silly show, one of Gran's favourites. I'd got up and gone to the bathroom, pink and cream and smelling of damp towels, and then into the kitchen, to sneak a slice of marzipan off the Christmas cake. I'd been quiet and careful with the cupboard door, knowing it wasn't right to steal food from my own Grandmother, that I could have asked, but I had a strange need to do it, a need to take the risk of being caught. And I remembered very clearly the fear when I'd suddenly felt aware of being watched. I'd frozen, trying to think of something to say, a way to explain why I was crouching in front of the dresser with my hands on the big green cake tin. A cold panic rushed through me from head to stomach and back again. I turned round, looking at the door, expecting to see Gran's face, angry, disappointed, lost; it wasn't her. It was Hector.

He'd stopped a few steps into the kitchen, his big white face turned up towards me, and stared without blinking, his feather duster tail slightly extended and still, except for a tiny twitch at the end. I knew he'd been trying to creep up on me, like in the game Grandmother's Footsteps, and had only stopped because I'd turned round. I stared right back at him, trying to intimidate him as much as he was doing to me, but he never even blinked. And then he sat down. Just sat down on the lino in the middle of the kitchen, as if he was saying, 'Hey, pal, I'm onto your game.'

From the living room came the horrible screech of audience laughter, almost hysterical, followed immediately by loud music which meant the end of the TV game show was near. Outside, in the vennel to the garden sheds, rain dripped from a gutter, and a neighbour pushed a shovel into a rattling mountain of coal. Hector didn't take his eyes off me. If I'd been in the kitchen to put away our supper dishes or fetch an aspirin for Gran, I would have moved. I'd have walked past him with no fear. But this was like school, when the bigger boys wouldn't let me go past them in the playground to reach the toilets. Not for any reason, just because they could, they were bigger, and they ruled. Hector was letting me know how things were in his house, and just like the scared and bullied kid I'd always been, I couldn't face it. I broke eye contact, looked at my shoes, around the kitchen. My stomach was tight, and the remnants of marzipan stuck in my teeth were too sweet, sickly sweet. My eyes felt hot and sore. I rubbed them one after the other. When I looked back at Hector he blinked once, got up, swished his tail and, calmly, turning his back on me, strolled into the living room. After a minute I followed.

Gran was still watching the show; the frantic finale was her favourite part, she liked to join in, calling out the answers the bouncy contestants were too confused or stupid to shout themselves. Lying on the seat beside her, in the place where I'd been sitting, was Hector. He gave me one long accusing look, and closed his huge, pale eyes. I wasn't worth his attention any more. Gran put out a hand and rubbed behind his ears. She turned to me and smiled, 'Well, Derek pet, shall we have a cup of tea? Fancy a wee piece of cake?' I went back into the kitchen and filled the kettle. When the programme ended, and Gran came through to fetch out the Christmas cake, I said I wasn't hungry.

The thought of that cake brought me back to the present. I'd had practically nothing to eat all day and my head was aching. The time on the video recorder said 2 a.m. There were digestive biscuits in the kitchen, I'd eat a few of them and head for bed. I turned off the lamp and yawned and rubbed my face and stretched, and as I got up I heard a small noise. A little clunk, the sound a light plastic box might make as it touches down on a wooden floor. It was too dark in the room to see the corner, too dark to see if I'd caught Steve. I reached out again to the lamp switch but just as my thumb touched the slide, I stopped.

That's when I saw how shortsighted I'd been. The whole Heath Robinson thing, the talc, the bucket, even giving Steve his name. And now the stalking, as if I actually wanted to catch him. That was the moment when I saw how I'd become so engrossed by the game I'd ignored the consequences. And in that fraction of time I saw myself the way you do in a dream. Prowling round in the dark, not as an average man in an average body, thin face, brown eyes, brown hair, pale skin. What I saw moved on silent padded feet, and as the head swung round into the moonlight, my eyes were huge and staring.

Acknowledgments

For 'Chuck Yeagering' stories in various versions, my thanks to Halla Beloff, Paolo Bazzoni, Chad McCail, William Gallagher, Amanda Hargreaves, David Johnston, Morag Joss, Martha Leishman, Chris Maguire, John McGlynn, Lucie Maguire, John McTernan, Siân Preece and Ian Willox.

To Philip Pullman and James Robertson, for their generosity in reading and commenting upon the whole lot, I am deeply beholden.

I'm grateful to *The Herald* and *Sunday Herald* for commissioning some of these stories, and to the BBC for broadcasting others; to the Scottish Arts Council for their support in the form of a writing bursary in 2001; and to my agent, Isobel Dixon, for skill and patience, ongoing.

Some of these stories have appeared on radio or in the following publications, in slightly different forms: *Mae West Optional* (the *Sunday Herald*); *Time Goes By* and *Her Drug of Choice* (*The Herald*); *Olympia* (Radio 4); *Under Observation* and *To Boldly Go* (Radio Scotland); *It's Good To Talk* (*Irishness in Scottish Writing*, Polygon); *Statutes & Judgements* (*Something Wicked*, Polygon).